UNDER MY BED

ROSE CHASE

Copyright

Also by

Volkov Bratva:
The Bratva's Bride
The Bratva's Beast
The Bratva's Bounty (10/24)

East Coast Syndicate:
Cardinal (8/24)

Serial Lovers:
Killer in the Sheets
Guilty of Love (TBA)

Content Warning

This book is a darkish supernatural romantic comedy that contains possible triggering/disturbing content.

Contents include (but not limited to): explicit language, violence, sexual scenes, sexual violence, abuse, alcohol and drug use, dub-con/CNC, BDSM elements and tones, mentions of assault, edge play (breath play, restraints), anal.

Listen, MMC is a shadow demon so there is going to be some shadow play.

If such content triggers you then please do not continue any further or skip areas of trigger!

Dedication

To those who want to fuck the monster/demon under the bed instead of fearing it. This book is cheaper than therapy, so here you go. Yes, the demon is a Shadow Daddy. And yes, shadows will be used in ways they should not.

Blurb

"OH, HE CAME WITH the house."

The first house I buy for a damn steal comes with an otherworldly surprise.

Needless to say, the housewarming I get from Kastoron is something less than magical.

Late-night talks and couch therapy sessions with the demon under my bed soon become the norm between us after I get used to his antics—he still gets me with a corner scare, though.

Who would have thought I would end up giving my soul to the demon who tried to scare it out of me on day one?

Then again, I never knew it was possible for a demon to adore me so much. Never did I think a demon would be the one to show me how to love myself for all I am.

Funny how we fear the shadows only to find comfort and pleasure in them.

Under My Bed

Umbra Demon Series Book 1

Rose Chase

Contents

Pronunciation Guide

- **Aesophedus:** Ee-soft-fee-dus

- **Amaldin:** Ah-maul-don

- **Kastoron:** Kas-tore-on

- **Levianth:** Leh-vi-anth

- **Tezrias:** Tez-re-as

- **Valphan:** Val-fawn

- **Zaesiel:** Zay-see-ale

Chapter 1

Kastoron

FRESH PREY.

It felt too fucking long since my last one, and even then, they weren't even amusing. Families were never entertaining, especially kids. An easy scare was always nice, but families were frightened too easily and got bland much faster than I appreciated. Also, kids weren't exciting to mess with. Some demons loved children, but I wasn't one of them.

Intrigue trickled down my spine at the smooth, melodic female voice saying, "But I'm curious, why is it so cheap?" By all things unholy, she sounded like a tempting siren.

It would be so easy to reach out and grab her right now. I wanted to feel her body tense up in my palms while her sweet screams filled my ears until my body melted with delight.

But if I wanted all that, then I had to be patient. If I scared her off now, I would never get the chance. I couldn't complain either; she was a very pleasing sight to my eyes. The last one had a nice pair of tits and an ass to die for, but she was filled with so much plastic that she was more of an eye sore than a beauty. Also, her voice was obnoxious. I liked tormenting others, not having it done to me.

"Oh, the last owners abandoned it, the city claimed it, and they are just having a hard time selling it because of the location." The real estate agent was more than eager to lie and omit many things about the property at this point, not that I blamed the poor thing.

No one in their right mind would willingly buy a known haunted house. Well, unless they were into that kind of stuff, which has happened in the past a few times, but they always got scared off in the end. Also, those kinds of people were annoying with always trying to contact me and asking me stupid ass questions about the dead, Hell, and shit. Oh, and that's not to mention the whole 'can you contact my dead mom, father, sister, grandma' and yada yada yada. Fortunately, they were easy to scare off, ironically.

"Is there anything wrong with it? I mean, it's a charming house for so cheap. Is it made from cheap materials or something?" I had to give this potential buyer some props for asking questions. Granted, they aren't the right questions, but at least she wasn't stupid enough to buy the place outright based on price and looks alone.

"I understand your hesitation regarding the home's listing price. However, rest assured, the property is constructed with durable, high-quality materials. Despite its history of changing ownership, it remains a reliable investment." The soft clicking of heels tapped at the air as the agent moved around. "Situated just beyond the city limits, it offers a serene environment. It's especially well-suited for individuals without school-aged children and minimal commuting needs."

Smiling a fake smile so bright, the agent spun around in a small flourished. "The expansive grounds provide endless possibilities for various activities. Additionally, the surplus rooms could easily be converted into a home office or photography studio. Furthermore, its remote location ensures fewer crowds and optimal natural lighting for your photography."

The rest of the agent's sweetened words droned on and on, but all I could think about was the potential buyer.

Why would she need to set up an office here? Did she work from home? If she did then that would be perfect because it means more access to her!

The last person that was here worked way too much and was never home.

Unsure, the human buyer sighed with a soft groan. "I mean, it all seems perfect for the price, but what's the catch?" Okay, I wished this person would be dumb enough to just accept the house already for the price.

Well, I wasn't sure about house prices or how that all worked because it's not like I browsed this 'internet' that these humans used. But from what this agent has been pushing, it was a 'steal' apparently?

"No catch besides what I have laid out." Liar. Too bad—for the potential buyer—the young woman couldn't pick up the agent's lie.

Releasing another sigh, the young woman seemed to ponder for a bit as she took a few rounds around the house, testing out every damn movable thing in the house to ensure it was in working order. At least the agent was truthful about this place being basically perfect because of the recent updates.

After a few rounds of the place, the human relented. "You know what? Fuck it. There is absolutely nothing wrong with this place. It's practically magazine perfect." Smiling a little warily, the buyer looked at the agent. "And I need my own place that could double as a nice ass studio, and some work in the backyard could turn it into another great place for shots. I'll throw in an offer."

Yes. Come to me, my prey.

I couldn't help myself from crooking a finger at her luscious, silver-dyed strands of hair, letting the smoothness slip across my demonic finger. Then, the temptation to tenderly caress her curvy body to map it into my mind twitched at my fingers. I wanted to trap her soft face in my hands, trace those sharp Asian eyes, and feel her plump cheeks and lips against my palm and fingers. Then, that soft-looking body of hers was such a divine temptation. I started to reach out, ready to give into the need for some physical touch, but pulled away at the last minute, causing a faint breeze.

"Hm? Strange, is the AC on or something?" The woman commented as she looked around with furrowed eyes. "Could've sworn I felt a small breeze."

"Must be kicking on again. Sorry, it was a little warm this morning when I came in, so I turned the AC on." The agent lied through her fake and nervous smile.

Too bad that won't be the only chill she will feel if she moves in.

Chapter 2

Stella

SOMETHING WAS DEFINITELY FISHY.

How the heck did a 2000-square-foot, three-bedroom, two-bathroom house, sitting on just over two acres of land, go for only five hundred grand? Especially out here in the sticks near Portland, Oregon, where places were selling for over a million bucks! Something was fishy, but I didn't give a flying fuck because I finally owned my own house—officially!

Probably not the wisest decision for a freelance photographer like me, but I could afford it because of the inheritance I got from my grandparents, and as long as my clients kept up like they have.

Oh well, too late now because I nearly went broke to get this place.

Speaking of my clients, I should probably start on that home studio sooner rather than later, but that could wait until tomorrow or the next day. I was too fucking exhausted after moving my shit out of storage today and setting up my bedroom.

A shiver chilled my spine again for the hundredth time it felt like today. This was strange because I had adjusted the AC, which should not be on now. It doesn't matter; I would be warm under the covers after I finished up my nightly routine and got cozy.

At least, that was the plan.

After cocooning myself in my sheets like a human burrito, I thought I'd fall asleep right away. However, I felt far from sleepy because of the eerie sensation that someone or something was watching me. A daring glance out the window showed no one—thank fucking god. Yet, the feeling never disappeared, even when I fell asleep from exhaustion.

Then, it began—the strange dream. Well, maybe it was more of a nightmare because no part of it felt pleasant. It felt like I was dreaming, yet still awake. Kind of like experiencing sleep paralysis, but I could still move. And the strangest part? The dream took place in my new bedroom.

Slowly, the edge of my bed dipped. I don't know what came over me to turn my head and look, but I did. Fuck did I regret it because the sight of the wispy black fingers of some monstrous-looking hand sinking into the mattress terrified my soul out of me.

"Lovely little thing, aren't you? Oh, we're going to have so much fun." Okay, that deep, raspy voice sounded too real—at least the fear felt real enough.

Creeeeeeak...

The sound of the bed giving way to this shadowy weight made my heart sink in my tightening chest as the thing crept closer to me.

It was a gnarly-looking hand—at least it looked very much like a hand—that stretched into an arm, or at least a good length of something. I didn't dare crawl closer to get a better look because I wasn't that stupid. From the looks of it, it came from over the bed somewhere, probably from underneath, because I saw nothing beyond my bed. The floor seemed clear, and I saw nothing strange coming from the closet.

Whimpering, I quickly ducked under my blanket, hoping it would be enough of a protection barrier. It was a childish hope, but I couldn't bring myself to budge any further from my bed. Besides, maybe the thing couldn't get past—

"Ah!" I shrieked in horror at the feeling of something curling around my covered ankle.

"That's it, scream for me, my little pet." The raspy voice chuckled darkly and tightened its grasp on my ankle before giving it a firm yank.

I couldn't control the terrified shriek that escaped me even if I wanted to. Instinct took over as adrenaline coursed through my body and kicked it into fight mode—which surprised me because I sure as hell thought I would freeze.

"No! Let go! Stop!" I had no idea what I kicked at because I still had my head hidden under my covers, but my legs flailed around, hoping to shake off whatever this was.

Unfortunately, it all seemed to backfire. "That's it. I love it when they fight." The thing sounded crazier with the excited laughter it released.

My struggling only seemed to spur it on more with how the grip tightened fully on my ankle and pulled until it was pinned firmly on my bed. Then, my other ankle didn't take long to join, making me lay flat on my back with my legs bent and spread wide.

Whimpering out a sob, I struggled against the death grip. "Why are you doing this? Who are you?"

Wake up! Wake up! God fucking damn it!

No matter how hard I blinked, none of it would go away. Either the world was cruel and not allowing me to wake up from this nightmare, or my imagination fucked with me evilly. God, I hope it wasn't the latter, though, because shit like this just didn't happen! Or at least it shouldn't even be possible; ghosts, demons, and all those things didn't exist!

A pressure against my chest caused my body and mind to jolt back to reality. "G-get off me!" For a shadowy thing, it weighed a crap ton. Wait, what if I had it wrong? What if it was some solid dark mass and not a shadow? Either way, it was bad for me, so I don't know why I should even ponder about any of it.

"Please, stop!"

Chapter 3

Kastoron

STUPID SHEETS.

I wanted her tears. I wanted to see the fear in her watery eyes before her sweet tears would cascade down her delicate little face, leaving the most perfect trails for me to lick up and savor.

But no! Here I was, fighting to get these stupid sheets off of her to get to my prize.

Unfortunately, my impatience got the better of me today. "Show me your pretty little face, pet, then I'll stop for tonight." Bargaining with a lowly human, how deplorable of me.

Yet, I had to resort to this out of sheer desperation. I couldn't remember the last time I had a human to torment, not like I kept track of the dates—it felt like a millennium to me. So, I had been itching for something—anything—at this point in time.

"No, please go away, please!" The human sobbed under me, her little body shaking like a leaf in a storm.

"Then show me your face, simple as that." I continued to press with a deviously deep chuckle. "Come on," I cooed, leaning down until my huge head hung above her covered one. "Just a quick peek. I like to see my pets."

"I'm not your pet!" She bit back with more snap than I expected, given the situation.

"The moment you moved into this place—no, the moment you decided to buy the place, you became my pet," I argue with a dark, toothy grin. "Now, be a good girl, and let me see that precious face. It's been far too long since I've had such a lovely lady to savor." Or, at the very least, a young and single one like her.

Slowly, I raked my elongated claws down the side of her covered face, causing her to whimper some more. I just wanted to see those pretty, glassy gray-brown eyes of hers. She was the perfect little thing. Even if her silver hair was unnaturally colored, it suited her young self.

Grinning darkly behind my shadowy mask, I held back my chuckle when I heard the rays of hope peek through her fear. "Promise you'll leave me alone if I do what you say?" Oh, how I couldn't wait to shatter it all.

"Yes."

For tonight.

She didn't need to know that. If she couldn't remember the nuances in my words in her little panicked mind, then that was her fault.

Relaxing, I eased off of her and had my shadow tendrils release her ankles, chuckling amusingly at her instant withdrawal. Pulling my shadow back, I made my massive body leaner.

I don't know why I was being nice to her like this, especially since I wanted to scare her and make her scream. She would probably still freak out quite a bit at the sight of my seven-foot-tall body towering over her. I wasn't bulky and ripped by any means, nor was I scrawny and weak; I was leaner and more muscular like most shadow demons of my kind. Of course, I could easily change my appearance using the shadows to add to myself, something I did more often than not for effect.

Even though I seemed more like my regular form, I still kept my features shrouded in shadow to keep up the eerie presence. It was too early to show my full face to her either way; that would have to be another scare for a different time.

Hidden under the veil of shadows, I let my lips stretch into an unholy dark grin as I watched her trembling hands lower the sheets until her scared and tear-stained face peered out from under.

Unable to help it, I reached out and delicately gripped her face to hold her still. "So fucking beautiful, if only you could see yourself through my eyes, little pet." The warmth of pleasure threatened to dissolve my hold on the shadows to reveal myself fully.

I wanted to press myself right up against her, feel her trembling body against my bare skin while I licked her tears away before making her cry more. Her round, upturned eyes made it so easy to see her glassy orbs that twinkled in the dimly lit room. Her high cheekbones glistened deliciously from her stream of tears, and her soft skin was silky smooth from the wetness of it all.

Maybe calling her a pet was a bit rude and undermining. After all, she looked so much better than some mere mutt on the streets. Calling such perfection something so low was ill-fitting.

"Such a perfect doll." My voice rasped against her cheek before my dexterous tongue came out and licked a trail of her tears. "So fucking delicious."

Such soft and fair skin wrapped around a shapely body. She wasn't skinny or thin, nor did she have too much. I love that she had curves and meat on her body. Her thick legs were nicely toned along with her arms, and I caught a very nice glimpse at her soft stomach earlier when she showered—a nice, curvy little thing.

"Please, let me go. You said you'd leave me alone if I came out." She whimpered through a small sob, her eyes purposefully avoiding mine.

"I never said *when* I would let you go," I remarked with a cruel smirk, lifting the veil of shadows a bit for her to catch it.

"You—!" The brief burst of confidence left as fast as it came when I narrowed my glowing amber-red eyes at her.

Chuckling, I curled a wispy finger around a lock of her hair that contrasted against my darkness so much. "The night is young and long. All I said was that I would stop for tonight, but I never specified *when* it would be tonight." The simmering anger under her fearful gaze was so adorable.

Feigning a disappointed sigh, I ran a curled finger down the side of her face. "Guess I can take some mercy on you tonight, given that it's the first."

Leaning in, I licked the other side of her face, making her whimper and shudder away from me in response.

"Good night, doll."

15

Chapter 4
Stella

NO MATTER HOW HOT I turned the water up or scrubbed myself in the shower, I couldn't get rid of the creepy feeling that somehow seeped itself into my bones.

Sleep was impossible after the thing slinked off the bed and disappeared under it. No matter how long I laid there in my comfortable bed, the creepy feeling of his...? I think it was a he. Pretty sure it was a male from the voice and lack of figure... Not like it mattered much at this point because he basically violated me.

The coldness from the creature's touch lingered long after it disappeared, and I could still feel its presence around me even though it wasn't physically present. It was probably this that made me think it was all a fucked-up nightmare still.

Maybe I'll wake up and feel normal.

That was just wishful thinking. Reality had its own agenda and decided to smack me in the face with everything, repeatedly playing it like a broken record. Then, the feeling of disgust crept over my body with waves of goosebumps until I felt utterly filthy. I couldn't stay in bed after my own mind and body got to me, so I booked it to the shower in the adjoined bathroom to scrub myself raw.

Which was where I currently remained because the scalding water gave me some strange comfort. Also, the bathroom was brightly lit, so maybe that would deter whatever that *thing* was. Or, at the very least, it might look less intimidating in the light if it chose to peek its dark, ugly mug into here.

Unfortunately, I couldn't stay in the shower or bathroom forever. I don't know how long I kept myself cooped up in the steamed-up room, but I instantly regretted it when I worked up the nerve to leave.

A small shriek of anger ripped out of my throat at the sight of my room. "You said you'd leave me alone!"

Seeing the thing—demon or whatever—sitting on my bed upon exiting the bathroom irritated me beyond belief, much to my surprise. I should probably be pissing myself out of fear, not feeling upset toward the damn thing.

"I am." Damn thing sounded so smug. I wouldn't be surprised if he had a smirk under all that misty black shadow mask of his. "I'm not bothering you, not touching you, not doing anything to you. Not my fault you didn't ask me to clarify my words."

I probably shouldn't talk back against this creature, but I guess I had a death wish tonight. "Can you do your own thing elsewhere that's not my bedroom? Or better yet, not my house." I snarked with a soft scowl as I steeled my nerves.

Whatever nerves I did work up ran away faster than a startled rabbit the moment he shot up from my bed and closed the distance between us in an instant. Stunned, I couldn't avoid his hand in time when he reached out and wrapped it around my neck. Then, a hard *thud* filled the room from my body being slammed against the wall. "Your house? *Yours*?"

The demon laughed in my face for a good second before tightening the grip around my neck and forcing my head up at him. "This place belongs to me, and it has been for centuries. The moment you signed your name on that stupid deed, you signed your life away to me." His seething words sent shivers down my spine as I tried—and failed—to shrink away from him.

"You are all mine now, so get used to it, doll."

Then, he released me and stepped back. "Be a good girl and get your ass in bed and sleep. Tired prey is no fun to mess with."

Yet, he made no indication of going anywhere. All he did was stand there, staring at me until it felt like my bones would crawl out of my skin. When it became too uncomfortable for me, I darted towards my bed and jumped into it. Immediately, my hands grabbed at the sheets and bundled them around my body, a silly way for me to make a stupid barrier between him and me.

"Would you relax? You're not going to get any sleep soon if you act like I'm some kind of monster waiting to kill you the moment you look away from me." He remarked with a curt laugh before he melted into the shadows under the bed and basically disappeared before I could quip anything back.

Chapter 5

Stella

IT WAS QUIET THE next morning, not a peep from the monster of last night. I managed to go through my whole morning routine in peace and even got some unpacking done.

As I was busy in my future home studio, I let myself get too comfortable with the peace—bad call on my part.

Okay, maybe it was a fucked-up nigh—

"Jesus fucking Christ!"

A stark coldness shocked my terrified body at the sight of a shadowy figure in the large mirror the moment I pulled the covering off.

Spinning around, I hoped to all that was holy out in the world that I hallucinated the damn thing, only to have it shattered in an instant when I found the figure to be standing a mere inch from me. Yeah, the thing was definitely real, which meant last night was very real.

"Aren't you supposed to be burning in the sunlight and shit?" I bit out with a snarl and stomp of my foot.

"I am a demon, not some stupid made-up vampire." He retorted with a scoff. "Also, they don't even burn up in the sun. Honestly, where did you humans even get that notion? And don't even get me started on the garlic shit, like out of all the things, garlic? Really? I mean, at least the holy water is believable." Well, at least his attention withdrew from me as he went on some tangent about us humans and our construed stories about supernatural creatures. Although, speaking about holy water...

Ah hah!

I knew I saw a bottle of it in the box by my foot.

Splash. Splash. Splash.

Stunned silence filled the room as we stood there staring at each other. "What the... Did you just... Give me that!" A violent swipe of his hand and the tiny plastic bottle of holy water was snatched from my hand. "What in Lucifer's domain is wrong with you, woman? And where the fuck did you even get this?"

"Okay... So holy water doesn't work on you either...?" Considering how he wasn't sizzling up, I would assume no. "And I think my mother threw it into my moving box." I didn't have any use for holy water, so why would I obtain some? Also, that was why I didn't mind wasting it on him.

The bottle hit me right in the face after he chucked it at me. "If it was real holy water, then yes, it would have worked."

"Damn, my parents will have a coronary then when I tell them it ain't legit," I remarked under my breath with a roll of my eyes.

Note to self: get legit holy water to get rid of the demon.

"Oof!" A winded grunt left me at the sudden shove from the demon that sent me to my ass. "What is your problem?"

Okay, maybe that was the wrong question because immediately, I was pinned to the wooden floor by vines of shadow that shot out of my own shadow under me. Then, bending over, the demon loomed over me darkly with narrowed eyes—at least, they seemed narrowed by how his glowing slits became smaller. "Nothing. This is just how I am." He laughed in my face before his shadowy hand ended up around my neck, choking me.

Panic quickly set in as my vision clouded and slowly dimmed. Thrashing my legs, I kicked at his—surprisingly—solid body while my hands clawed at his arm. "No! Stop! Don't kill me, please!" I gasped through my struggling breaths.

Yet, the heavy curtain of unconsciousness never came. My vision blurred to almost nothing, my mind clouded over from the lack of oxygen, and obviously, I struggled to breathe because of the hand around my throat. But I never reached the cusp of passing out. If anything, the closer I came to the point, the more his hand loosened until he held my neck loosely in his grasp.

Growling, he shoved his face up close to mine, making me yelp and turn my face away in fear. Deep laughter filled the air as I felt his body shake above me. "There we go, that's what I wanted." His voice was right next to my ear, the depth of it causing me to shiver with the slight tingles of pleasure that pricked at my body.

"Y-you're sick and twisted." I whimpered through an airy exhale. "Why don't you just go haunt someone else."

"Because this is my domain, and you happened upon it. I am going nowhere, so either get used to it or scram along like the others so my next meal can come." His words snapped at me like a bite, making me flinch a little as I fought against the restraints.

"W-wait, you're going to eat me?"

Is that what happened to the previous owners? Holy fuck, what did I get myself into?!

The demon's body shook again as his head threw back in a laugh. "Oh, Lucifer, no, I'm not a completely carnivorous demon. Besides, you humans taste nasty, like a mouthful of rotten corpses." I couldn't tell if he was serious because I couldn't see his expression. He sounded like he was joking, but only God knew the truth at this point.

"You know, this might be the start of something new for me, doll." He mused with a chuckle, his hand tapping my cheek. "Won't change the outcome for you, but I'll have much more fun."

"Fuck you!" I spat at him with angry eyes as my struggle increased.

"Oh? Sorry, but I don't sleep with humans." He shot back smugly with another laugh, making my face heat up red. "Besides, that's not the kind of screaming I want from you."

Gritting my teeth, I let out a frustrated grunt and let my body go completely slack.

There had to be a way to get rid of this fucker, and I intend to find out how.

Chapter 6

Kastoron

1 week later

She's doing it again.

I don't know why, but I didn't like her looking at those stupid pictures of men or her stupid pictures. Yeah, it was her job, but I still didn't like it because she was too focused on all of it instead of me. I mean, I probably should let her work so she could make money to pay for the house and remain in the house. It didn't mean I liked it, nor would I leave her alone.

"Hey!" She shouted in protest when I turned off her computer monitor. "I was working you asshole."

The gall on this human, I swear, I otta...

Scowling, I gritted my teeth, formed some ropes with the shadows beneath her, and used them to tie her down to the chair. "And I don't like that. I don't like that you are ignoring me, you insolent human." I seethed inches from her face. "And you better watch that tongue and mouth of yours with me."

"Or what? You'll keep bugging me? You know, I can leave you alone and just work in my rented office. I thought you'd appreciate my presence and be less lonely." She snapped back sarcastically with a shaky breath.

Growling, I flicked a finger at her, and another shadow rope instantly wrapped itself around her neck and choked her. "You will do no such thing." Looming over her menacingly, I let my eyes trail down her bound body to waste some time. "If you don't start behaving how I want, then you'll find yourself in new predicaments that will keep your mouth occupied." An empty threat, but she didn't need to know that.

As fun as it would be to see her struggle to breathe while being choked or having my fingers shoved down her throat, I wasn't the type of demon to be that cruel in retaliation. I might be a demon, but sexual assault was way below me. I much preferred my victims to be willing. That and the aspect of them breaking and giving into me was much more tantalizing.

Some demons got off on that shit, but some, like me, didn't. Not all demons are horrible monsters like humans tend to think of us.

Yeah, I might be a big asshole to this female human, but most of the time, it was harmless fun. Most I've ever done so far was leave some bruises from throwing things at her and maybe from grabbing her a little too hard. Well, that was the most I could do to her in terms of harm because of damn restrictions from the witch that played me.

Taking a deep breath, I leaned down and grabbed her face, squishing her round cheeks together. Then, I couldn't help but smile a little out of satisfaction when her eyes chilled over with apprehension with the movement of my thumb across her bottom lip.

Slowly, her eyes softened with curiosity as her eyebrows raised a little. "Do you have a body? Or are you just a shadowy thing?" Her words were almost incomprehensible because of how hard I gripped her face.

"Yes, I only hide myself like this to look more scary to you." I don't know why I bothered answering her stupid question. She didn't need to know about the muscular body I hid beneath this shadowy veil, nor did she need to see my blueish-gray skin. "No more stupid questions," I growled sharply, causing her to flinch as a spark of fear sparkled in her eyes.

It's been about a week since she's been here, and she's managed to grow a backbone. Yet, it was satisfying to see how I still struck fear into her. It would be utterly dull if she adapted fully because then I might actually be bored to death.

However, I had to give her praise where it was earned. Out of all the humans who had lived in this house, she was one of the very few who got somewhat used to my presence sooner than later. If my memory served me right, she might have been the only one besides one more who had adjusted well. The other few were already mentally ill and saw demons before they happened upon me, so I wasn't going to count them.

Looking back at her monitor, I turned the screen back on to reveal the image of a half-naked man. "Why do you even take such pictures of people? The stupid weddings and happy mushy couples I get, but why those sexual ones? Isn't that what porn and the internet are for?" I asked out of sheer curiosity.

Taking a deep breath, she looked at the screen with appreciative eyes. "They're not for that kind of thing. Pictures like these, boudoir pictures, they're meant to capture the beauty of the individual. Everyone has their reason for doing it, but I love doing boudoir sessions to help people gain that boost of self-esteem. Sometimes, people don't see what others do, and I love showing them that other side because many don't realize just how gorgeous or sexy they look from another's point of view. It's just a beautiful art on its own, and it's hard to describe the joy of it all."

"You humans get weirder and weirder by the centuries. I remember when it was so scandalous to show your damn ankles." I remarked with a mocking scoff.

"Ew, you sound old as fuck." She joked with a snicker.

And you're fresh, young prey. So ripe and perfect.

Chapter 7

Stella

2 months later

"Wait, there really is no way to get rid of him? Are you sure?" I hated the defeated desperation in my voice, but I really did feel deflated after hearing what the paranormal investigator told me.

"I'm sorry, but it would seem that he is bound to the house at the very least. Unless you are willing to bulldoze and burn the place and the grounds to ashes, he remains. A priest can't help you here either because the demon is just too old and powerful." Offering a frank and apologetic smile, they placed a hand on my shoulder. "I'm sorry, but the best thing for you to do is move while you can. I don't know of the demon's full intentions or how dark they are, but he doesn't plan on letting you live in peace while you are here. Usually, my advice and methods for protection might work, but it won't work in this case, given the demon's power. I really am sorry, but this conclusion is as much as I can give you."

Unfortunately, the comfort didn't last long because the investigator's hand went flying off with the sudden appearance of a shadowy figure. "Leave before I throw you out of here myself." The demon seethed in a deepened and raspy growl.

So much for being a hardened investigator, the man took off faster than a startled rat at the demon's threat.

Unfortunately for me, I wasn't free to go.

A winded grunt squeezed out of me in response to the demon slamming and pinning me down on the couch. "You dare let another man touch you? You're lucky I didn't paint the walls of this place a nice shade of blood red just now." He seethed inches away from my face as the shadows from under the couch crept up and tied my body down.

"What is your problem? You won't leave me alone, constantly pestering me, continuously breaking my shit, keeping me up at night, and giving me no peace." Pausing, I breathed deeply to keep myself from fully exploding. "That man was doing nothing to you, nor is he important to me. He was just trying to give me some comfort about this shitty situation." With a frustrated sigh and yell, I glared at him with all the anger I could muster. "Do you really want me to suffer so much that you won't allow me one second of peace and comfort?"

The demon was quick to snap back at me. "You can get your stupid comfort with your ice cream and stupid stuffed animals, not from some stupid, insolent man who had bad intentions towards you. You have any idea what he was thinking about the whole time he was here? If anything, you should be thanking me for throwing his ass out of here or be begging me to teach him a lesson."

"Wow, a demon with some morals and honor, lucky me." I bit back sarcastically with a roll of my eyes.

Gritting my teeth, I hissed from the pain of him gripping my face and wrenching it around to face him fully. "You should count whatever blessing and miracle you have that I am not like the low-level demons." He growled at me, pressing me further into the couch. "If I was, then you would either be dead or my plaything until you wish for death."

Without a response in my mind, I bit my tongue and scowled at the demon instead. "What are you even doing with me?" Honestly, I wanted to know because this damn thing confused the ever-living fuck out of me.

It's been about two months since I moved into this place, and this demon began tormenting me. He had become rather annoying at this point in time rather than terrifying. I mean, I was still scared of him somewhat because he was a damn demon at the end of the day and held powers incomprehensible to me. He could easily kill me—thankfully, he hasn't tried—if he wanted.

Still, he gave me no reprieve, always popping out of the blue and giving me jump scares nearly around the clock, throwing my stuff around, knocking things over, nudging me awake at night, and he's even gone as far as tripping me and dragging me around using the shadows.

For the most part, he irritated me. It was usually only the first few scares that got me when the day would start or during the night when he would literally pop out of nowhere and shove his face right up to mine. If I had more guts, I might have tried to punch him a few times for his lack of personal space.

"Whatever the fuck I want because you are mine, and don't you forget that." Shivers ran down my spine at his possessive words, and a small concern nagged at me because of how much I enjoyed his words.

Yeah, I might be fucked up in the head a bit for somewhat liking the attention from the despicable demon. At least someone out there in the world cared enough to give me attention every day—even if it was the wrong kind of attention.

I really need some therapy.

Groaning internally, I threw my head back against the couch and stared up at the ceiling until the demon loomed his face over mine. "Like I said before, better get fucking use to me." His smug chuckle made me want to lash out across his face with an open palm.

I hated how he was right, but I would make him eat his words. I was stuck here with him, but fuck that. The tables will be turned; it will be him that has to put up with me. I threw nearly everything into this house, so unless I declared bankruptcy and shit, moving was not an option unless I wanted to end up homeless or back with my parents.

I refused to be terrified and tormented in my own home.

"What's going on in that pretty little head of yours? I don't like that look in your eyes." He sounded a little wary of me, which he should be.

"Thought you could read minds." I retorted with a snort, earning a growl and another face grab from him.

"Don't lash that tongue back at me. I can only read the minds of those vulnerable or wicked. Your head is too filled with rainbows and cupcakes for me to invade." His irritated demeanor changed as he let go of my face and fully leaned up to his knees. "Besides, it probably doesn't have a single thought in it."

"But it has something you want to know about and can't figure out. Otherwise, you wouldn't have asked." Arguing with a demon was probably not the best choice, but oh well, at least it was fun.

If I have to live with this fucker then I would have to pull my big girl pants on and own this shit.

Better fucking buckle up, buddy, because I'm gonna drive this fucking shit show.

Chapter 8

Kastoron

1 week later

What in the circles of home is she doing?

Why is she so fucking calm about all of this?

Okay, maybe she just didn't like that vase and wanted to get rid of it. I'll just break this new one she got. That otta get her riled up enough.

A premature smile of victory stretched at my lips as I picked up the new vase she'd set out on the display table and chucked it at her. Only to have her completely ignore me!

What the actual fuck!?

Clearly, the thing hit her because I heard the soft impact of the solid material against her back, and she did make a small grunt. But why didn't it break or throw her off balance? I threw it with enough force to jar her, yet she acted as if something merely bumped her lightly. Then, the stupid object had the audacity to not shatter upon impact with the hardwood floor.

Okay, if I actually thought about it, the vase felt a little off in terms of weight when I picked it up, but most human things felt like nothing to me.

But the vase *bounced* on solid ground.

Then, here was the kicker: she continued with whatever the fuck she was doing.

She didn't even spare me a single glance.

In a fury, I appeared behind her after grabbing the vase again. This time, I raised the thing up high and threw it down on her head because I physically couldn't whack her with it. But once again, the damn thing basically bounced off her and clattered to the floor in one piece.

Bewildered, I picked up the thing with a scowl and inspected it closely. "What the..." Gritting my teeth, I grabbed the human by her shoulder, and spun her around to face my furious face. "Human, explain this sorcery," I demanded.

"Maybe if you address me properly and ask me nicely, I might." Why this little... How dare she use such an innocent tone with me and demand such a thing from me? Actually, how dare she even demand anything of me.

Who does she think she is?

Letting my anger seep on with my growl, I grab her by the neck and pin her up against the hallway wall before shoving the vase into her face. "What did you do to it." I wasn't even asking yet again.

The scent of fear permeated the air briefly before disappearing completely with her little snicker. Now, that pissed me off because this was no laughing matter. Nothing about this should be amusing or funny. Also, how dare she laugh at me!

Pulling her away from the wall, I slammed her back against it with another growl, causing her head to thump against the hard surface with a pained grunt. "You better answer me before I lose my patience with you." She was damn lucky I couldn't kill her or do too much harm to her. Stupid wards.

"Or what? What will you do? Throw my dinner in my face? Knock the plates off the counter? Turn my TV off while I'm watching?" The nerve on this human. Where the fuck did it come from!?

I didn't like her standing up to me. It wasn't supposed to be like this.

"I'll just spend a longer time at the studio and do my work there, so you don't shut off my computer in the middle of my editing. Maybe I'll even put out an ad for more male boudoirs too since—oof!" I did let her finish by pulling her off the wall and slamming her again.

"If you dare look at another naked human male, I will hunt him down and tear his stupid appendage off and fuck you with it." Okay, I wouldn't do that, but I had to make a threat to scare her.

Also, I don't know why, but the thought of her looking at other men made my blood boil with rage. No, I wasn't jealous—I couldn't be. Me, a shadow demon prince, jealous of a pathetic human male who had nothing against me? How fucking ridiculous. I just didn't like her looking at other males, especially ones with little to no clothes on.

I mean, watching her edit those stupid photos of hers already made me angry, which gave me more reasons to shut her device off when she was working on such things. I already didn't like it when she did those stupid photos with families and shit because they had men in them, so those stupid male boudoirs or whatever the fuck they're called really grated my nerves the wrong way.

Laughing softly with a smile of disbelief, she looked up at me. "Oh my God—"

"Do not bring him into this." I groaned with a roll of my eyes, not that she could tell because, again, my face was hidden with a shadowy veil—it always was.

"You're jealous. That is so funny." She snickered with an amused little smirk on her face. "What? Afraid I might leave you for someone who can actually do something to me? Someone who isn't an annoying little brat vying for attention? Someone—mhmmfph!"

What. The. Actual. Living. Fuck.

Chapter 9

Stella

HOLY FUCKING SHIT.

What do I do? What are you supposed to do when a demon fucking kisses you!?

Do I kiss back? Am I supposed to kiss back? Was I allowed to kiss back?

I mean, did I want to kiss him back? It wasn't a bad kiss... Not that I would admit that out loud to him because he didn't need the ego boost or anything like that. But damn, this kiss got better and better by the second.

Before I could definitively decide, the warmth of his lips escaped me along with his presence. "What the... Hey! I didn't kiss back... Demon, come back!" Great, I didn't even know his name to summon him, if that's how it even worked.

Letting out a frustrated shout and huff, I crossed my arms. "You're such an asshole!" I shouted into the air, hoping he heard me.

Grumbling to myself, I picked up the plastic vase to set it back on the table before going back to replacing all my breakable things with plastic versions of them. Yes, I had to replace all my nice dishes and bowls with damn plastic ones. I didn't mind it too much; it just kind of looked a little tacky, but hey, it beats shelling out money every other day to replace things because the demon decided to be a toddler and empty out my cupboards.

Even though I kept myself occupied, I couldn't help but think about what happened. Never in my life would I have expected something like that, mainly because I couldn't see or read his damn face. So, I could never tell what went on with the demon. Let me correct myself; I never saw anything besides his crazed grin or smug smirk when he showed it to me. Other than that, I had no idea what the rest of his face looked like. Wait! What if he didn't have a face?! What if that's why he kept it covered? No, that made no sense because he had a mouth... Unless the mouth was some creation?

No, the mouth was real. I felt his—surprisingly—deliciously soft lips against mine just earlier. I couldn't lie, demon or not; his lips felt amazing, and so did his taste. It sounds kind of gross, but he tasted a little ashy...? Stoney? Mountainy? It's as if the smell of fresh rain was a taste; that's what his lips tasted like. Or maybe he just tasted like a rock, who knows. Either way, I liked it, and I wanted more.

I just had to be patient; my chances would show up sooner or later. There hasn't been a day that's gone by without him popping up every other hour or so. Actually, I don't think he's ever gone a full twelve hours without doing something.

Most of the time, it was harmless. Actually, now that I thought about it, all he did was relatively harmless. I mean, throwing objects at me might not seem so, but he never threw them hard enough to do real damage. Most I've ever gotten from his antics were a bruised ego and physical bruises. Well, and a scare, of course.

No matter how accustomed I've become, him appearing out of nowhere around a corner or in a mirror if I looked away and looked back still got me sometimes. Yes, he still managed to startle me, even if I anticipated it nearly every second.

No matter, adapting to him wasn't an issue for me, but I still had to figure out a way to deal with him if I wanted to turn the spare room into a studio as I had planned when I bought this house. Eventually, I wanted to do photoshoots at my own home to save money on a studio rental. Plus, if I had my own private studio, then I could buy and use whatever furniture I wanted and needed without consulting anyone else. Unlike now, where the studio I rented was shared with a few other artists, everything we did had to go by vote and a schedule. Oh, and I could finally have a fully open schedule!

The main reason why I searched for a house instead of an apartment was because I wanted to run my own studio out of the place, and I wanted to have a space to call my own that I actually owned.

This place was perfect and more than what I could ever hope for. I mean, it would have been perfect if it didn't come with an unwanted roommate who spent every hour of every day tormenting me with childish antics. He probably wouldn't be so bad if he were a nice demon. Actually, could demons be nice? Or decent? Or would that go against their nature?

Sighing, I ran a tired hand through my hair to put it up in a messy ponytail. "Hey! Do you want dinner?" I usually didn't ask him, but I felt he might not devour whatever food I made tonight. I didn't want to make extra and leave it there to spoil.

It was silly to make food for a demon, but he started it. I made some food once, and when I turned around to grab something, he gobbled the whole thing up without a word. After that first incident, he always ate my food, like *all* of it. So, I had gotten into the habit of making a second serving or some extra for him to have, which he always ate.

SLAM!

All the drawers and cupboard doors in the kitchen opened and slammed shut simultaneously.

"Oooohkay..." I lightly clicked my tongue as I cautiously moved around my kitchen to prepare some dinner for myself. I didn't set out a second serving this time, though, because I assumed the slamming doors meant a big 'no' in response to my question. There was some extra, but I packed that into the fridge for tomorrow, or possibly now, if he decided to devour my dinner when my head was turned.

Fortunately, dinner was quiet tonight for me. Not gonna lie; it felt kind of sad and lonely not to have him poke at me or pull my utensils away from me while I ate.

It was even more disappointing when I didn't see him appear in the bathroom mirror after I wiped the steam off of it after I stepped out of the shower. I actually frowned a little when my eyes were met with only my reflection. All the scares probably weren't good for my heart, but the little jolt here and there was a nice way to feel alive again, unlike now, where it remained in a steady rhythm.

With a sad sigh, I settled myself into bed after drying my hair. I should probably be happy about having some peace ever since I moved in. Yet, I couldn't help but worry about the demon and when I would see him next. I mean, there's no way he could have actually run off for good, right? It was just a kiss—one he initiated out of the blue.

The sound of shuffling and scratching against the wood brought an eager smile to my face, and my heart raced with happiness at the sounds of my sheets rustling and the bed dipping a little.

Not wasting another second, I spun around to face the edge of the bed, where a shadowy hand crept its way onto the bed.

I don't know what came over me, but my hand instantly shot out and grabbed the demon's hands, intertwining my fingers with his and death gripping him.

Quickly, I hung my head over the edge where the demon's head started to peak out from under and met a pair of widened eyes.

"What's your name?"

Chapter 10

Kastoron

...

The human touched me. She touched me! She fucking reached over and grabbed my hand!

This has never happened before, a human making the first contact—especially this boldly. I wanted to grab her and scare her some to get myself back in my groove after I made the mistake of kissing her earlier. Well, I don't know if I would classify it as a mistake because it definitely didn't feel like one.

The whole thing still confused me, if I was being honest. I literally don't know what went through my ancient brain to get me to that point. I had no intention of kissing her, but my mouth found hers before I could process a plan of action.

Her reaction to my antics irritated me because they were not what I expected or planned for. Then, her replacing everything around the house with stupid plastic to ruin my fun really ticked me off. I wanted to strangle the life out of her for being so insolent, but I couldn't kill her. So, guess the next best thing my raging mind thought of was the kiss.

That damned kiss.

I had to pry myself away from her before I lost control and tore her clothes off at that moment. It hurt my pride a little to hide from her—a stupid little human. If any of my brethren found out about how I ran and hid after kissing a human because I was terrified of the feelings it brought on, then I could kiss my shadow prince's status goodbye for good.

I didn't think a simple kiss would crack open some tomb of fiery desire for more. I wanted to absolutely devour her the moment I got a taste of her. I wanted to run my hands down her plush, curvy body and grab ahold of her love handles. Then that juicy ass of hers, they were more than enough to fill my big hands. I wanted to show her just how lovely her body was.

Speaking about her body...

Slowly, I slinked out from under the bed and onto it. "Tell me why you keep starving yourself, and I'll tell you my name." I bargained in a cautious voice.

"Excuse you? I don't starve myself. I eat three full meals a day." She remarked with a pouting scowl.

"You barely eat three decent meals a day." I corrected her with a roll of my eyes. "I can see you eying my portion of the food or the ones you set out for the next day. For someone of your size and stature, and considering your work, you need more than what you portion yourself."

Probably another strange thing this human did was leave food for me. Granted, I didn't really *need* the food, but it was nice. It felt like forever since a human made a meal for me to enjoy. Well, at this point, it probably has been forever. The last time anyone willingly fed me was when I was first summoned.

"I'm not that hungry. I don't have much of an appetite most of the time." Such a crafted lie. Too bad I could see through it like a sheer veil.

Sighing, I eased my form to seem a little smaller as I scooted closer to her. "Human, quit lying to me. Those stupid words might work on others who don't give a shit or don't know any better, but you can never deceive me."

"I have a name, you know." She grumbled with a soft glare at me. "It's Stella."

"And I don't remember asking or wanting to know." I snarked back, not liking how she took the initiative. Sure, I might have been a little curious, but I wanted to know on my terms. At least her name wasn't too bad.

"You still haven't told me yours." She nudged at my shoulder with a poke of her finger.

Sneering, I lightly smack her hand away. "And you still haven't told me why you starve yourself." I could play this game all night.

"Promise you'll give me your name?" She asked in a wary voice and unsure eyes that furrowed together.

Groaning with a roll of my eyes, I nodded. "Yes, you annoying woman."

I expected an answer right away, but she hesitated momentarily with tightened and pursed lips. "Like I said before, not that I am starving myself because I still eat my three meals a day. I just eat what's needed to slim down." She admitted almost shamefully.

"That's a load of bullshit. Slim down? Why on this green earth would you need to do that? You are perfectly fine how you are, and more importantly, you appear healthy." Sure, she might have a little extra tummy, but it wasn't even that much.

Not that I would admit it to the damned human, but I found her perfect, curves and all. Honestly, though, she wasn't even that much overweight or anything, so I have no idea what went on in her stupid little head. If I didn't have much restraint, I'd tie her down and use her plush thighs as a pillow to nap. Then that juicy ass, damn, I wanted to grab and grope them, sink my teeth into them, and Lucifer, they'd look so wonderful jiggling from a nice spank.

And I was more than willing to bet she was a nice cuddle, too. She'd fill my arms quite nicely, and her soft body would feel like a cloud against mine. Actually, she would probably feel like a lovely teddy bear, like those obnoxiously huge ones human males liked to get their woman on Valentine's Day.

"You should take your own advice that you tell your clients, love your body as it is because it's beautiful and shit. Don't be one of those hypocritical idiots." I scoffed softly with crossed arms.

"They look beautiful. I, on the other hand, look icky. I'm just a little chunky and chubby and need to lose a few pounds or twenty." Her voice started to trail off towards the end, making me reach over and grab her face.

The shadows that hid my face fell away fully to show my stern expression to her. "You. Look. Perfect."

"Holy shit, you look hot." I don't think she realized what she said because she continued to stare at me with those awestruck eyes. Then, she even went as far as touching my face.

I didn't like to be touched, but I wasn't too bothered by her soft hands. So, I let her hands linger on my face. Although, I couldn't help but chuckle a little in response. "Not all demons look horrendous or have a face that not even their mother could love."

"Well, you always have your face covered, and I didn't know why. I mean, you could have been hiding some deformity for all I know." She remarked with a roll of her eyes before she went back to trailing her fingers over every inch of my face and ram-like horns.

Fluttering my eyes shut, I let myself enjoy the feeling of her soft fingers working down my forehead, over my prominent eyebrows, down the high bridge of my nose to my full lips. "I still need a name for this handsome face." She giggled cheekily as she traced my sharp jawline.

Rolling my eyes, I reached my hands up and reluctantly removed her hands from my face because I didn't like the warm fuzzy feeling blooming in my chest from the contact. "Kastoron." I reluctantly answered her.

"Kastoron..." She tested my name out on her tongue a few times before looking at me with pursed lips, which had me tilting my head in response. "I'm gonna call you Kassie."

"I beg your fucking pardon!?"

Chapter 11

Stella

HUMMING TO MYSELF, I happily moved about the kitchen to make breakfast for the day.

Thud!

Instinctively, I ducked my head and avoided the jar of salt that came flying at me from across the kitchen.

"Kassie, that's not nice. I mean, I needed the salt, but you could have handed it to me nicely." I chided playfully, not even bothering with looking around for Kastoron, who I knew at this point constantly lingered around me.

A low growl ripped through the air before he physically manifested before me and threw me against the kitchen counter using the shadows under us. "Would you quit calling me that!? It's such an insult to call me such a girly nickname!" He snapped with a soft glare and scowl.

"Okay, that's just rude because Kassie can so be a guy's name. No such thing as a boy and girl name in this day and age. This is an all-inclusive home, mister, so none of that shit. It's the 21st century, and we accept everyone and everything." If his stupid shadow tendrils weren't holding my hands down against the counter, I would wag a finger in his face.

Stunned, he blinked silently at me a few times before releasing me fully to lean in and trap me against the counter between his strong arms. "Excuse you? What century now?" His face hung inches from mine as he raised an eyebrow.

"Twenty-first," I replied in a confused voice.

Well, I never thought it was possible for a demon to have that mid-life crisis look on their face, yet here Kastoron stood, stunned as hell. "Unholy shit... Are you serious? You're not joking with me?" After I made no indication of proving him wrong, he groaned exasperatedly and pulled at the two black ram-like horns that protruded from the top of his head. "Satan's ball sack. I've been in this damn place for five centuries!"

Pursing my lips in thought, I looked down at my hands and tried to do the math in my head but failed horribly. "Uhh how many years is that?" According to my failed math, that would have placed him in the 16th century or so.

"Five thousand years, give or take. Lucifer's halo, I didn't think I'd been trapped here that long." He grumbled with a scowl.

I was about to make a comment about his age because, to me, that was ancient, but the last part caught my attention more. "Trapped? What do you mean?" He didn't seem trapped with how freely he moved around the house and did stuff. Hell, I've even seen him outside on some occasions, and he has followed me outside, too.

"Kassie." I poked at his chest, trying to get his attention to no avail. "Kassie, don't leave me hanging. What do you mean by trapped? You move pretty freely last I checked."

Mumbling something under his breath, he shook his head at me before grabbing my face and bringing me up into a breathtaking kiss. Just like two days ago, I was frozen with shock at the sudden action. We haven't done anything like this since that one incident days ago.

Even after our little light-hearted conversation that night, we didn't exactly go in one direction or another. Kastoron was still a little asshole to me with his antics of taking my shit and hiding it, throwing things at me, knocking things over, jump scaring me, typical stuff for him at this point. Although, things between us have shifted a little in an odd direction. I mean, he kept up his antics, but he also became more present around me when I was home. He had no concept of personal space before, but now his presence felt more suffocating when he would crowd around me. Oh, and he actually showed his face around me now; no more hiding it with the shadows unless he was trying to give me a jump scare, but then the mask came off right after my reaction.

Either way, I still didn't know what to do in this stupid situation—one I never thought would happen again. Do I shove him away? Engage in the kiss? Was it even right for me to—fuck it.

Leaning in as much as I could, I eagerly returned the kiss with a shaky inhale through my nose. Now, I half expected him to pull away and disappear like last time, but he surprised me by grabbing my hips and pulling me flush against his body. Then, the feeling of something prodding at my lips had me gasping, letting whatever it was slip in.

Of course, just when things might get good, he pulls away. "What did you do to make yourself taste so alluring?" He groaned against my lips before running his long tongue against my bottom lip.

"Nothing... But why did you kiss me again?" I asked in a small voice as I struggled a bit against the shadow restraints.

I wanted so badly to hold him, place my hands on him, and explore every inch of it. He was huge, seven-foot-tall or so, with a muscular, athletic build that suited him quite well. Also, I'm pretty sure if he looked like some buffed-out gym rat, then he would actually look terrifying and menacing.

"I don't know. You were just too tempting." I couldn't tell if he was lying or not, but he sounded genuine enough. "And I let my curiosity and anger get the best of me."

"Curiosity? About what?" I pressed with interest. I mean, what could a demon like him even possibly be curious about? Especially if he was *that* old, shouldn't he know nearly everything by now?

Kastoron opened his mouth but quickly closed it and shook his head. "It's nothing. Forget about it." The lustful air around us quickly turned heavy as he leaned back and released me.

"Kastoron... You can tell me. And what you said before about being trapped, what did you mean by that?" Now that the feeling of his lips didn't cloud my mind, I could fully recall our little conversation from before.

Unfortunately, seems like I wouldn't be getting an answer. "It's nothing, forget this happened. Go back to making breakfast, and I expect you to actually eat a full meal to your heart's content like yesterday, or I will fuck up your day so bad that you'll be pulling that silvery hair out of anger." His stern words came out in a flurry before he disappeared completely, leaving me alone in the kitchen.

What is his problem?

Chapter 12

Kastoron

1 week later

"You missed a spot."

A cry of frustration came from Stella, followed by a smack to the shower curtains. "Quit perving on me!"

"Well, if you didn't have such a delicious body, then I wouldn't." I teased with a chuckle before sneaking a shadow tendril under the curtain and up her leg. "You should take it as a huge compliment. I don't spend my time in the shower with any prey unless they're really worth it."

The only thing that would make it better was if I was actually in there with her to physically see and feel her luscious body in my rough hands. I wanted to feel every inch and burn it into my mind. Well, I could do that if I really wanted; not like she could stop me from throwing the curtain aside and joining her naked glory.

"Ugh!" The sound of water splashing followed the image of her figure stomping. "Kastoron! This isn't fair! You can't just touch me like this."

"Says who?" I retorted with a playful edge to my voice.

"It's my body, my choice, and it feels weird to be touched there." She replied with a soft whimper; no doubt her lips were in a pout right about now, too.

"I'm only touching your inner thighs. I gotta make sure my pillows are nice and clean." I didn't see what the big deal was because it wasn't as if I was touching her breasts or pussy.

"It's weird, don't touch my chubby thighs. They're disgusting." I hated how my gut twisted at how sad she sounded.

"Did I say they were disgusting? No, I didn't, so who did?" I asked, feeling a little peeved at the fact someone or something out there put such stupid thoughts in her mind.

"Growing up, a lot of people, particularly my family, always picked on me for being more on the chubby side and looking like a little roll." She replied in a hesitant voice.

A heavy sigh was heard from her before more words followed, "My family never gave me a break, from my parents to aunts, uncles, and cousins—nothing. Being anything over a hundred pounds in an Asian family and you get reamed on to no end. It was one of the reasons why I went extremely low contact with my family after I moved away for college and got a taste of a nontoxic environment." Her voice trailed off into some stupid mumblings about how she still heard people around her talk shit about her body.

Before I could stop myself, my body pushed itself off the bathroom counter and approached the shower, where my arm threw the curtain aside, startling Stella. "Kastoron!" She gasped, throwing her arms around herself and shying away from me. "Get out! I'm naked!"

"And I don't give a shit," I growled while eying her hungrily.

One big step was all it took to fully back her up against the shower wall, where I caged her in between my arms. "The only thing disgusting about you is how little you think of yourself, how you put yourself down, how you keep trashing this beautiful body of yours along with your attempts to change it, and I was going to add in the fact that you are a feeble human, but that's not fair to you because you can't change that fact."

"But—"

Oh, for fuck's sake!

Fed up, I leaned down and kissed her hard with a deep groan. Pressing my body fully into her, I fully sandwich her between me and the wall before grabbing her hips and pressing them into me so that she could feel the raging hard-on I had. "I may be a demon and fucked up, but disgusting things don't turn me on." Carefully, I rolled my hips into hers, running my covered length—I always kept the lower half of my body covered with makeshift shadow bottoms or a shadowy mist—against her puffy pussy lips. "This is what your wonderful body does to me."

Running a hand up her body, I grabbed her face, "This cute, round face with the softest cheeks." Then, I trail my hands down to her small breasts and grope one, "These cute little tits." Groaning, I slowly ran my hand along the curve of her waist and rested it on her love handle, "These fucking curves and grabbable hips. You have any idea how many times they've plagued my mind?"

Sucking in a sharp breath through my gritted teeth, I slipped both my hands around her back to her ass. "And this juicy fat ass of yours, fuck, it drives me crazy watching this squeezable and slappable ass jiggle with every step you take. And when you wear those jeans." I had to pause to let out a guttural groan. "Fuck." Recollecting myself, I lean down and rest my forehead against hers before looking deeply into her darkened eyes with my own. "Then these thighs of yours, so plush and soft, so perfect."

Hooking my hands under her thighs, I hoisted her up and wrapped her legs around my waist. Then, just as she opened her mouth, I silenced her before she could get a chance to utter a single sound. My lips descended on her in a devouring kiss full of unbridled lust. Her muffled protests hit my tongue as I invaded her mouth and took claim to every inch of her. "I am going to show you just how much I love this fucking body of yours," I growled against her lips before going back to kissing her hotly.

"A body like yours deserves to be worshiped and loved, not berated and hated. Those people who make fun of you, tell you to shave a few pounds off, say unsavory things, all of them, they need to all fuck off, and you need to tell them to fuck off because you are perfect just the way you are."

Chapter 13

Stella

I ALWAYS HAD ISSUES with my own body growing up, and I still did.

Call me a hypocrite because I rave to my clients about loving themselves and all that shit, but I never could bring myself to that point. I didn't *hate* my body, just a very strong dislike. I didn't like my thick thighs, my little stomach pudge that always muffin topped over my pants, the same stomach that gave me soft rolls, and I really disliked my ass that I could never fit into jeans.

"Kastoron." My fear chilled the air as I looked up at him. "I don't know if I can do this," I admitted shamefully, turning my head away as I tried to dislodge myself from him.

Much to my surprise, his grip on me tightened, and the shadows under us rose and wrapped around our bodies, anchoring me to him. "I can smell your arousal and feel your heat. If you're afraid that I will be rough, then I can assure you I won't. I am going to adore and spoil your body." Well, wasn't that just sweet of him.

Sighing heavily, I shook my head, still refusing to meet his gaze and taking an interest in counting the tiles of my shower instead. "It's not that I'm not turned on and don't want you... It's just... I can't... I just... Can you just please put me down Kassie, please?"

For a demon, he was drop-dead gorgeous and sexy as fuck; even a blind person could see that. Kastoron's athletic, muscular body was built for sin. I loved how he wasn't overly bulky or muscular, just toned enough to where the outlines of his muscles were almost a soft touch to his body. For a demon, he looked real.

He felt real enough to. I couldn't help myself from reaching out and tracing the contours of his muscles, starting from his collarbone to those lovely pectorals of his down to the deadly six-pack abs. Then, oh Lordy, his v-line was to die for with how perfect the dip led to his illegal tool.

I wanted him, I really did, as crazy as that sounded, but I didn't want to be hurt or ruin this growing relationship of ours–whatever this fucking relationship was. And no, I wasn't talking about the awkward after-sex relationship. I didn't want to have sex with him because sex wasn't fun.

"Oh, come on, please don't tell me you're one of those wait-until-marriage kind of person?" Kastoron scoffed with a roll of his eyes as he released the shadows from around us. "But no, I won't put you down right now."

Then, despite my protests, he removed us from the shower and took me to bed, where he—surprisingly—gently laid me down. I didn't appreciate the fact my sheets were now soaked because of our wet bodies, but I couldn't make my displeasure known to him because his lips distracted me.

"Answer my questions, doll." He muttered against my lips after breaking the heated kiss.

Swallowing the lump in my throat, I turned my head away from him to hide my reddening face. "I-it's not what you think. I'm not a virgin or someone who wants to wait until marriage, no... It's just... I don't find sex good, and it's painful." That was the embarrassing truth to it all.

Glancing up at Kastoron, I frowned and worried my bottom lip between my teeth as I waited for his mocking laughter or some kind of equal response. Instead, the look of amusement that quickly turned into a concerned one surprised me.

Letting out a deep breath, he sits up entirely and pulls me into his lap as he leans his back against the wall. "What do you mean, Stella?" His dexterous fingers rake through my wet strands, separating them.

"Sex just doesn't feel good. I don't know how else to put it." I really didn't because even my own body confused me. "Like it's fine all up until the actual sex part usually, but sometimes it's the in-between stuff, too." The thought of my past experiences flashing through my mind sent a shiver of disgust down my spine.

"Stella, doll, talk to me. Explain it as best as you can." His deep, raspy voice was so tender that it was hard not to melt into him.

My stomach churned until dinner threatened to come back up. "I don't know... It's just sometimes, with kissing and foreplay, it feels fine, but I guess I get cold feet or something when it comes to having a dick shoved in me. The few times I did have sex, it just felt raw and painful, and it just made me feel so icky in my chest." I wish I could offer him a better answer, but that was all I could manage of the truth.

"Sounds like you didn't have much luck in partners then." His dry chuckle only made the sick feeling in my stomach worse for some odd reason. I think he caught onto my discomfort because his face softened again with grave concern.

Those enchanting red-amber eyes of his morphed into a harsh rage as he studied me closely. "Wait, were you raped?" He seethed through clenched teeth.

My mouth immediately opened for an answer, but nothing came out. I shouldn't be struggling; the answer should have come out without hesitation. Others have asked me before, and I always gave them the same answer of 'no' without thought. However, no one has ever asked me such words as Kastoron point blank.

"Stella, doll, answer me." He seemed so angry yet so broken and concerned.

But why?

It wasn't my fault, none of it was, so why is he angry at me and looking at me like that?

Chapter 14

Kastoron

IT HAD BEEN SO long since I felt the burning inferno of rage like this, but seeing the broken realization cross Stella's frowning face made the volcano inside me erupt.

"I-I wasn't raped... I got into bed with him, I kissed him, I let him kiss me, touch me..." Lucifer's halo, she sounded like a broken record with her response, and it pained me a little on the inside.

Sighing softly, I grab her falling head to keep her attention on me. "Did you want to have sex with the man? Or woman?" Hey, I wasn't one to judge, even if she did chide me a little about the little nickname the other day at breakfast.

"I-I don't know? Yes?" Her soft voice cracked with her frown as she began to curl herself up.

Holding her tightly, I lowered my head and rested it against hers so our eyes were leveled. "Stella, it should never come out so unsure. I need to know, Stella, did you or did you not want to have sex with that person? I don't care if you consented to kissing and touching and getting into the room with the person, but the actual sex itself, the part of having someone insert their private part into you, did you want and agree to that wholeheartedly?"

Stella remained concerningly quiet in my arms for a bit before shrugging her shoulders in response. "I don't know."

"Then it's a no. There's no such thing as being unsure or not knowing when it comes to consent, Stella. It's either yes or no, no in between. If there is ever a time when you start to feel unsure about something, then it needs to stop or pause." No wonder the poor thing didn't like me touching her much.

I felt like such a little bastard now, too, after knowing.

Carefully, I laid her down in her bed and got on top of her before kissing her deeply. "I might be an asshole to you, but I would never harm you like that or dare toy with such an idea." It was one thing to chuck a plate at her face and see her get flustered or endlessly poke at her until she snapped, but *never* would I ever violate her as such.

"Let me show you how amazing it's supposed to feel, please." Begging a human for sex, yeah, this was definitely something I never thought I'd be doing. "I promise I will stop the moment you say so, and if you ever want me to stop or feel the slightest discomfort, then I need you to tell me."

"What if I don't like it? What if it hurts again?" Fuck I wanted to hold her tight and make her fears go away for once rather than feed them.

"If you don't, then you can let me know, and I will stop. I'm not going to lie. It will hurt when I slide my cock into you because I'm not exactly human-sized down there." Judging from her size alone, it was a no-brainer that she would struggle to take me. No pun intended, I had a monster—demon—cock.

"C-can I see? Your dick?" She asked with a red flushed face that she tried to hide with her pillow.

Chuckling, I easily whack the pillow away with a shadow tendril. "Don't let it scare you," I warned her before letting my pants dissolve away from me, letting my member slap down against her stomach.

Tensing, she leaned up onto her hands. "Holy shit!" She gasped with wide eyes and a gaped mouth.

"For one, shit can't be holy." I laughed softly as I watched her gawk at my cock that probably looked like some monstrous dildo from a sex store or specialty site.

"Oh my God, you're going to kill me with that thing! You are not putting it in me." She protested with a stammer, her eyes still locked onto every inch of my glorious length.

Following the dip of my V-line and over a tuft of pitch-black hair was my long and thick cock that was easily the length of her arm from the elbow down at least, and it was definitely too thick for her to wrap a single hand around the shaft that was lined with ridges from the crown to base. Yeah, my cock might look strange to a human or something out of a made-up porno, but for us demons, having a 'strange' cock was normal.

Using a shadow tendril, I wrap it around her wrist to bring her trembling hand to my monstrous member. "Touch it, it won't bite you." I snickered teasingly. To urge her some, I tugged at her wrist using the shadow wrapped around it until she was a mere inch from my twitching length.

Gritting my teeth, I sucked in a sharp breath with her soft hand wrapped itself around my shaft and stroked it nervously. "I won't put it in you tonight if you really don't want to, but I still want to show you pleasure in other ways." Smirking, I let my long tongue slither out of my mouth, making her gasp and bite her bottom lip to hide her growing smile. "I can't wait to feast on your delicious cunt." Just the scent of her arousal alone drove me up the wall.

Her round eyes widened as her cheeks flushed again. "Wait, you don't mean... You're actually going to put that on me? Isn't that disgusting?"

Grinning, I leaned down and licked the full length of her neck and cheek. "Oh, doll, haven't I told you from day one how delicious you taste?" I teased with a chuckle before kissing her deeply with a groan. "I am going to feast on your cunt until you can't give me any more orgasms," I promised her with a growling grin.

Slowly, I kiss my way down her body to her delicate breasts and grab both of them in my hands. "So soft and perfect." I hummed with a satisfied smile, kneading her mounds until she squirmed under me with the softest sighs of pleasure. Her softening eyes remained apprehensive as she watched me lean down and take a hard nipple into my mouth with a soft groan.

As much as I wanted to be rough with her, I knew I had to take it slow for now. I didn't mind it; it meant more time spent with her precious body. I needed her to relax around me and actually lust for me until all that would be on her mind was me and my cock pounding into her with no mercy.

Patience though, time and patience, and I would have her on her knees for me.

Pulling off her nipple, I quickly created a pair of hands with the shadows and replaced my own with them so that her breasts and nipples would be constantly stimulated while I kissed and felt my way down her curvy body.

"I'm not like whatever pathetic wimp of a human male you've been with. I know how to appreciate and worship every inch of a female's body."

Chapter 15

Stella

"OH MY GOD!"

The feeling of his big, long tongue pressing against my aching sex shattered me with immense euphoria.

"Do not bring him into this, I do not need a cock-block right now." He grumbled against me before placing his mouth over me completely.

Oh God!

I couldn't help but buck my hips at him when he began to suck and lick at me, giving wave after wave of mind-numbing pleasure that I had never felt before. Reaching down, I tangled my fingers in his long black locks and grabbed at his horns, eliciting a grumbling growl from him that sent vibrations to my clit. "Doll, if you do that, I'm going to eat you out like a depraved demon." Peering up, I could see his darkened eyes that had a crazed hint to them.

Giggling, I offered him a half-apologetic smile before stroking a teasing finger down the length of his horn to the base of it. "T-that feels so good. I want more, please."

What the hell had I been missing my whole life? My only ex-boyfriend never wanted to go down on me and made it sound like such a disgusting act. Yet here I was with a very eager demon between my legs, licking every inch of me and sucking at me like I was some juicy apple. And my God, did it feel divine.

Shuffling his head, Kastoron used his horns to nudge my legs further apart before anchoring them down to the bed using shadow ropes. Heat instantly filled my cheeks at the sight of myself being spread wide for him to have as much access as possible. Then the feeling and sight of his hands trailing up and down my inner thighs—oh fuck I was in trouble.

"Kastoron!" I gasped sharply at the feeling of his muscular tongue pushing inside my tight walls.

Unable to help it, I gripped at his horns and pulled him closer with a deep moan as I felt my stomach tighten. It ached, and I wanted it to stop. But I didn't want him to stop for the sake of relief. "Kastoron, it—oh fuck!" Before I could let him know of my pain, the feeling of his finger rubbing my clit along with his tongue in me and his shadow hands toying with my breasts and nipples became too much.

Whatever tension built up within my stomach snapped, and all I could do was let out a strangled moan that turned into a silent scream as my mouth hung open with my thrown-back head. I didn't expect such rapture to consume my body from the painful ache hitting its threshold, and my mind turned blank trying to process it.

"Kastoron!" I nearly screamed through my whimpering as I sobbed from the overstimulation.

The demon didn't let up. All he did was smirk at me with his eyes before pushing me further off the edge until I screamed his name again. Only then did he ease up and sit back on his knees with a cocky ass grin as he licked my juices off his face. "I'm more than willing to bet no one's ever gotten you to orgasm like that." He snickered with a cheeky grin before leaning down and kissing me roughly. "Fuck, I could really spend all day between your beautiful thighs if it meant getting drenched in your addicting juices." He groaned against my lips.

His taste and scent, mixed with my juices, filled the air around us and overwhelmed my senses. I realized how wet they had gotten from him when he pulled away, and the air chilled my lips and cheeks. "Why are you so wet?" I managed to stammer out in my haze.

"That was all you, Stella." He chuckled softly before capturing my lips again in a hungry kiss. "You went off like a broken faucet once I found your sweet spot and kept stimulating it."

Horror chilled my body at his words, and my hands instantly went up to my face to hide my embarrassment. "Oh my God, I am so sorry!"

The sinking feeling in my stomach only worsened at his light laugh. "Oh, doll, I think it's a little too far gone now to be sorry to the big man upstairs." I wanted to cry and hide under the bed now—and I did manage to do the first.

"Wha? Hey, what's wrong?" Kastoron's voice immediately softened with concern as he scooped me up into his arms and lap, using the shadows to pry my hands away from my face. "What's wrong, Stella? Talk to me."

Biting my bottom lip, I looked anywhere and everywhere but him. "It's so embarrassing, and you're laughing at me." I sniffled.

"Okay, now I'm a little confused, doll." He sighed in defeat as he pulled us both down onto the bed. "What's embarrassing about me teasing you a little?" He asked after he situated me on top of him.

Leaning up onto my forearms, I prodded at his chest with a nervous finger for a few seconds before peering my eyes up at him with a soft frown on my face. "I just peed all over your face, and you're laughing and teasing me about it," I admitted shamefully.

At this point, I started to wonder if he took some kind of twisted pleasure in my shame and misery because he burst out laughing again, which made my frown deepen. "Quit laughing at me." I snapped, my hands slapping uselessly against his shaking chest.

"Oh, Stella, doll, you are too cute and precious." He said between his dying laughter. "I'm laughing at your sweet innocence and obliviousness to your own orgasm." He clarified with a calming smile. "You didn't piss on me or anything like that. You squirted, which is a type of female orgasm that not many can achieve. Even if they can, it usually takes the right kind of stimulation to get a female to that point. So, the fact that I got lucky with you being one and getting you to squirt so much kind of stroked my ego."

Well, now I felt embarrassed about the fact that I knew nothing of my own body and pleasures. Also, I was embarrassed by the fact that this was technically the first orgasm I ever had, now that I really thought about it. I mean, my ex gave me some pleasure, and I thought he got me to orgasm a few times because the pleasure did reach a height. But *never* did my ex give me something remotely close to Kastoron.

And the scary thing was, I liked it.

No, correction: I *loved* it.

And I wanted more.

Chapter 16
Kastoron

A TWISTED SMILE CURVED at my lips at the sight of her eyes darkening with want. "Still want to continue?" I asked sweetly against her lips with a smirk as my hands palmed the globes of her ass.

Her wary eyes trailed down to my hard member pressed against her stomach. "You're not gonna fit, though. You're huge." She whimpered with a disappointed frown.

Chuckling, I quickly flipped our positions so she was back under me. "I just asked if you were ready to continue, nothing about if you want to continue with my cock." Even though that was the end goal, she definitely needed more preparation.

"Y-you'll stop if I say?" Her nervous eyes desperately searched mine for an answer.

Reassuring her with a smile and nod, I leaned down and kissed her softly. "Yes, but come up with a safe-word real quick before we continue."

A small, cheeky smile broke on her snickering face before she tried to cover it up. "What about God?"

Okay, I couldn't help but chuckle a bit at that one. "If that is what you want, as long as it's a word you can remember fully and use without hesitation." Although, I had to give her props there because that word would definitely catch my attention. The big guy upstairs won't mind. I mean, everyone else uses his name all the time, so being a safe-word won't hurt him.

"God it is, since he seems to bug ya little." She chuckled softly before grabbing my horns and pulling me down into a heated kiss.

"Doll," he growled against my lips deeply, "Pull my horns again, and I won't be responsible for your inability to think and walk tomorrow."

They might not seem like it, but my horns were really sensitive. Demon horns weren't meant to be functional—no, we didn't use our heads as battering rams—but more for display. Don't know what went through the mind of whoever created that aspect of us, but it was stupid how sensitive they actually were.

"Spread your legs for me, Stella," I commanded with a light nudge with my hand.

She was quick to obey and spread herself wide for me. "Good girl." I purred with a smile.

Sitting back on my knees, I took a good moment to burn her gorgeous body into my mind. The slight movement from her arms had me summoning ropes of shadow to tie her hands and arms down to the bed. "Don't." I bit out with a displeased scowl. "Don't you ever hide your lovely body from me ever again."

Reaching out, I ran my thumb up and down her wet slit, getting the digit coated with her juices to smoothly rub her swollen clit with the pad of my thumb. "Breathe, relax." I reminded her when her breath hitched and picked up at a nervous pace.

Slowly, her tense body relaxed into the bed as her hips bucked at my hand. "I am going to slip some fingers and shadow tendrils into you, stretch you out a little so that you can take my cock easier, alright?" Gently, I circled the tip of my middle finger around her entrance, teasing her while I waited for her answer.

She whimpered with a nervous bite of her lip. "Just go slow, please." With a shaky breath, she looked down at me warily but warmly with trust-filled eyes.

Smiling warmly back at her, I leaned down and kissed her deeply and slithered my tongue into her mouth to distract her. Breaking the kiss, I stifled a groan behind my gritted teeth as I slid my finger into her and felt how tight she was. Good fucking thing I didn't go straight for the grand prize because I would have ended up a damn loser with how I probably would have blown my load within a few thrusts.

Burying my face into her neck, I nipped around the slender column until I found the spot that made her squirm and sigh with pleasure. Without hesitation, I latched onto the area as I slipped a second finger into her tight channel and worked her open more. Carefully, I sank my teeth into her neck as I sucked harder and harder until I came close to breaking her skin. Only then did I pull back with a proud smirk when I saw the lovely mark on her neck.

Can't wait to see her reaction when she finds that later.

I couldn't help but snicker to myself a little at the thought of her freaking out at the large hickey on her lightly fair skin.

"How are you feeling so far? Wanna call for the man up top yet?" I teased with a cheeky grin as I added a third finger, causing her to gasp sharply as she came around my digits.

Sighing out a breathy moan, she rolled her hips at my hand. "Your fingers are so big, and it burns. But fuck, it feels so good. I don't want you to stop."

Deciding to push her a little, I slither two shadow tentacles the size of my finger into her stretching pussy and continue fucking her in tandem with my fingers until she moaned out another orgasm.

Keeping the tentacles in her, I withdrew my fingers and locked my eyes with Stella after forcing her gaze on me with a grip on the face. Smirking, I slowly licked and sucked my fingers clean while Stella watched me with wide eyes full of surprise and wonder. "Fuck I shouldn't find that as hot as I did." She shuddered with a blushing smile.

Slowly, the tentacles retreated until the tips were holding her pussy lips open. "Fucking delicious," I growled under my breath before trailing my eyes down her spread body to her twitching cunt.

Opening her legs further with the shadow ropes, I settled close to her dripping sex and grabbed my aching cock, rubbing the tip and full length of it along her juices to lube myself up before positioning my tip at her tight entrance. Even if I did stretch her a bit with the finger and shadow fucking, this was still going to be a tight fit.

My eyes snapped up to hers, searching her wary face to see if she had any second thoughts. Then, the moment her head nodded, I pressed myself inside of her with a soft groan. "Shit." I hissed out a growl as I gripped at her plush thighs. "Fuck you're so fucking tight." Maybe I might just break her in half.

Carefully, I studied her twisted face, slowing my pace down to a complete stop when I noticed the pleasure in her eyes flee with her tears. "Shh, shh, it's okay, Stella. You are doing so amazing taking me. So good. Breathe, baby, breathe, and relax." Keeping a shadow tendril curled under her chin, I refused to let her glimpse down at my monstrosity splitting her in half—unless I wanted her to freak out and possibly put a stop to this, of course.

A good portion of my length remained unsheathed still, and I was pretty sure that if she saw how much there was left to go, then she would freak the fuck out. Yes, I had every intention of getting all of myself into her. No, it won't kill her, not while I had the protection spell going on her.

My abilities might be severely handicapped because of the wards placed on this prison of mine, but at least the person who summoned me gave me the privilege of performing useful and harmless spells and tasks. That would be something to bring up with Stella another time, the wards, I mean.

Right now, I had a perfect woman to screw stupid after I fully stuffed her.

Leaning down, I gently licked and kissed her tears away while soothing her with sweet praises to ease her nerves more. Carefully and slowly, I moved my hips in small thrusts to get her used to the sensation while I inched myself in bit by bit. "That's it, doll, just relax and take me all in like that. Good girl." A little over halfway now, and her face wasn't scrunched up in pain anymore—I considered that a lot of progress.

"Fuck, it hurts so much, but I don't want it to stop. This feels too good." She groaned through a trembling breath, her hips thrusting softly at me. "Fucking magical."

"I know my dick is pure magic." I joked with a chuckle, making her giggle and laugh softly in return.

The words hung on my tongue, but I couldn't let them slip to her ears. Stella wasn't the first human I have fucked, but she was definitely the first to feel this amazing—and not because I haven't had sex in a long ass time. This really did feel magical, as stupid as it sounded. Even though I barely fit in her, this moment felt very fitting—ironically.

Truly, I have never felt this before, ever.

And it scared the demonic life out of me.

"Kastoron?" Her usually melodic voice chilled me to my very core because it was a stark reminder of my current situation. "Move. Please."

Well, can't deny a sweet plea like that. I'll just fuck her and get her out of my system and go back to terrorizing her tomorrow.

With my mind set, I gripped her hips tightly and picked up the force of my thrusts to force in the last inches until she was completely impaled on my dick. "Fucking perfect." I couldn't help but admire the splendid sight of her pleasure-filled face as I ground myself into her.

"If only you could see yourself right now, such beauty." Then, a thought crossed my mind that got me chuckling. "You know, I should have stolen one of your cameras and captured this moment for all of time."

Giggling, she looked up at me with mischievous eyes. "Next time, we can explore that more, but right now, I need you to fuck me, please." Smiling sweetly, she bucked her hips at me to urge me.

Just fuck her and be done with it. Fuck her out of your system.

I reminded myself before tightening my grip on her—she'll probably have some bruises there tomorrow. Pulling back until only my tip remained, I waited a teasing second with a dark smirk on my face. "Kastoron." She whined with a whimper. "Ka—AH!" I couldn't help the dark laugh that escaped my grinning face when she screamed at me, thrusting fully back into her.

The room was filled with the most obscene moans and screams of pleasure, along with the sounds of my prick moving in and out of her over the next few moments as I wrecked her poor cunt with my thick length. "Enjoying sex now?" I asked teasingly with a knowing smirk.

"Yes, amazing, fuck, you're ruining me, and I love it." She sputtered between her moans. "Your cock is so amazing."

"Damn right, it is." I laughed haughtily while picking up the pace. "You're never going to enjoy a pathetic human cock after tonight. Gonna be a little demon cock whore after this." The feeling of her walls clamping down on me at my words had me straining out a groan. "Oh? You like that, doll? To be a little demon cock whore?" Just like before, her soft walls tightened around me.

"Yes, I want to be your little cock whore." She moaned happily through her blissful orgasmic smile.

My cock whore. Fuck why do I love the sound of that more than I should? More importantly, why do I want that?

Shaking my head, I threw my thoughts away and shut my mind and feelings out. I shouldn't think or feel anything for her. She was just a craving I needed to kick.

I growled softly in a deep voice as I picked up my pace until the bed was crashing against the wall from my thrusts. "Come again, Stella, come again one more time for me." Her poor body would have been jerked so violently if it weren't for my shadows anchoring her.

A few more thrusts, and she was sent over the edge. Throwing her head back, her mouth hung open in a silent scream as her body tensed and trembled under me from the shocks of her orgasms. I couldn't hold back this time as her pussy clenched around me in a vice grip. So, with a loud groan, I buried myself to the base inside of her as I emptied my load into her greedy cunt.

"Kas-tor-on." She stammered out between her strangled breaths as her body shook from the aftershocks of her orgasm.

With a wave of my hand, all the shadows around her body disappeared. Leaning down, I quickly scooped her into my arms and laid down on the bed with her on top. "Such a good girl, you did amazing," I whispered against her temple as I peppered it with kisses.

Absent-mindedly, I stroked at her long, soft locks that contrasted against my pale, dark blue-grayish skin—almost like the moonlight against the night sky. This moment was... Sweet... And shouldn't be happening. I should be retreating under the bed right now, leaving her to clean up the mess of our activities, not holding and soothing her. Nor should I be making any attempts at caring for her. I don't know what came over me, but I controlled an arm of shadow to fetch her towel from the bathroom and slipped it under her.

Groaning softly, I carefully removed her from myself, shivering and smiling delightfully at the sight of my cum gushing and dripping out of her used pussy. Yeah, now I really regretted not stealing her camera for pictures because that was a sight I wanted framed forever.

Using the shadow arm, I cleaned her up and settled her next to me before taking her water bottle off the nightstand

and making her hydrate some. "Sleep, Stella doll," I murmured against her lips before ghosting a kiss over them.

I don't know what compelled me to stay, but I held her in my arms until she fell into a deep slumber.

Then, like a cowardly one-night stand, I slipped away from her and went back under to the darkness of the bed's underside.

Chapter 17

Stella

"KASTORON!!!"

That fucking shithead demon—I'm going to kill him!

The bathroom filled with his amused chuckling snicker, but his face never showed. "Something a matter, Stella doll?" It sounded like he was beside me, but I didn't see his reflection in the mirror.

Turning around, I searched the room for him while clutching the towel tightly against my freshly showered body. "You asshat! How the hell am I even supposed to cover this damn hickey up!?" Yeah, it was very hard not to notice the row of teeth indentation around a large purple spot that ate up the whole junction of my neck and shoulder! I knew he was pretty occupied with the area last night, and I felt the nipping and sucking. But I thought he left little love bites, not one big chomp!

"It's not even that bad." He retorted with a laugh, making me let out a frustrated groan. "You're working from home today anyway, so you'll be fine." His dismissive voice trailed out and disappeared along with his presence.

"Kassie?" Disappointment deepened my frown when I got no response and only felt emptiness in the air. "Kastoron?"

It was highly unusual of him not to be around me. Even if he was quiet, his presence lingered, and I could feel it. But not this time. For the first time since I moved in, I truly felt alone.

And it hurt.

Had I done something wrong?

Okay, that was a ridiculous thought because I literally just woke up and wasn't even finished with my routine after our passionate night together. So literally, I couldn't have done anything to grate his gears enough to warrant this cold shoulder from him. Unless he got pissed off at me saying 'good morning' to him when I woke up, which I think not because he replied with a swat to my ass along with a laugh.

What is his problem?

It couldn't have been about last night, right? Everything went amazing. At least it felt and seemed like so. He didn't complain or make any snide comments about us sleeping with each other last night. Speaking of which, the damn jerk snuck out on me during the night. It saddened me more than I cared to admit when I woke up to an empty bed.

His arms felt so strong and nice, and I loved how safe they made me feel. I wished he stayed next to me the whole night. Sure, waking up to a demon's face would be something new, but I was used to Kastoron. So, his ugly mug—okay, he's not actually ugly—wouldn't have been a huge shock to me.

Maybe he just needs a break.

Putting him aside in my mind, I went about the rest of my morning before settling at my little office area, which I had set up in a corner of the living room. Slowly, I worked through editing the photos of the latest wedding I did, all while peeking over to the dining room table where a plate of breakfast sat waiting to be eaten.

The house had an open floor plan, which I absolutely adored because I loved the space and seeing nearly everything from any place in the house. It also gave Kastoron only so many corners to scare me from—he still got me most of the time, though, because jump scares from corners were scary! Honestly, not gonna lie, I wished he would peep his head around the corner right about now.

Sadly, he didn't answer me when I asked him about breakfast. And I still couldn't feel him around me. The peace to myself was nice, but I grew rather bored and lonely faster than anticipated. I even found myself just calling out for him in hopes he would show up to get some kind of reprieve from this empty pit in my chest.

Kastoron had grown on me after all this time, so the thought of him leaving me after all this time and showing no indication was like a knife to the heart. Then the fact this happened after our special night together, where I opened myself to him and gave myself to him fully when I have never done so to anyone else. I let him have me, and he gave me the best night of my life—probably the best I will ever have.

It sounded stupid, but I felt something special form between us. If I was being honest, I felt some kind of spark from the first time he kissed me. After my shock of the situation died down and I had time to fully process everything later on, I couldn't deny that his lips on mine sparked some kind of inferno alive within me.

I felt a strong desire for the monster under my bed, and last night was a moment of clarity for me. When I came down from my orgasmic high, reality crashed into me like a boat crashing into an iceberg. I craved Kastoron, badly.

This fire in my soul flared to life because of him, and I needed him like how I needed water and air to live. The desire and need for him were insane and impossible to deny after last night.

Honestly, I didn't understand any of it because how could I have fallen so hard for someone I disliked strongly until the time he first kissed me three(ish) weeks ago. I barely knew the demon still after that first intimate contact between us. We bugged each other and got back to our usual routine of him fucking around with me—not like that!—and me either spoiling his antics or giving in to them.

Besides that, we never spent time with each other, so we knew little to nothing about each other. The only thing I knew about him was that he lived under my bed, had free roam of the house and property, could use electronics (found this out the hard way after he fucked up one of my laptops), ate whatever food I made and set out for him (except for this morning), and he liked to be around me a lot of the time.

Chapter 18

Kastoron

2 days later

I can't take it anymore. I need her. Now.

Two fucking days was my limit. How pathetic.

It killed me to cold turkey her, and I honestly thought I could kick her from my system if I ignored her and kept myself away from her.

Yeah, worst idea of my whole existence.

If I could remove myself from the damn place, then I would, even if it wouldn't help in the end. Fully removing myself from under the bed, I stood at the side of the bed and loomed over her with narrowed eyes.

I don't know how much time passed before I reached a clawed hand out and stroked her soft hair as she continued to slumber peacefully. The temptation to weave my fingers through the fullness of her hair and grip at her silky locks to pull her head back and shove my—

Fucking unholy realms of home, stop! Don't fuck with the human, literally.

But by Lucifer was she hard to resist. Having her sleep in her bed right above me every night but not being able to touch her nearly drove me insane. I couldn't hold back anymore tonight, obviously because I was touching her. I needed a hit. I sounded like a damn addict, but that's what she felt like to me.

Something about that first night—no, that first kiss!—broke something within me. And it terrified me because I have never felt such intense feelings towards anyone in my life, even to my first and only love. The reason why hung at the back of my mind, but I swatted it away like an annoying imp because I refused to accept it.

I should be leaving. Go back to hiding under the bed. But I couldn't help but lean in and trace my tongue along the length of Stella's succulent neck. Yeah, bad fucking idea because tearing myself away from her after that was impossible.

Growling softly, I crawled onto the bed and hovered over her like a starved beast as my lustful eyes carved her sleeping figure into my mind. Stella was dressed in a silk nightgown that had ridden up to show the curved bottoms of her juicy ass, and the plunging neckline shifted to where one of her nipples threatened to slip out. Pair her outfit with the way her body delicately sprawled out as if she was offering herself to me, and my urges became too much to resist.

Hands of shadows crept onto the bed and took hold of Stella's body until her gown was pulled down to reveal her perky breasts to my hungry gaze. Then, slowly, I had thin tendrils wrapped around her breasts and nipples to squeeze and tug at them softly.

Softly, Stella stirred but never woke, and I couldn't help but mentally scold her for it. How the hell was she supposed to defend herself against an offender if she didn't wake easily?

Stupid human.

But she's my stupid human.

Fuck, there I went again. She wasn't mine. Well, she was, but she couldn't be. And if I knew what was good for both of us, I would be sure to keep it that way. After tonight, of course.

Sitting back on my knees, I watched as the shadow tentacles I created slithered up her legs while some more shadow hands hiked her gown up around her waist to reveal—

What the fuck!?

Smack!

Stella startled awake with a sharp gasp as her body jerked up from my sudden slap to her exposed pussy. Her wide eyes nearly bulged out of her head when they landed on my scowling face. "Kas—ah!"

Stella's mouth hung open with pleasure at the sudden intrusion from two of my fingers hooking into her tight walls. "Why the fuck aren't you wearing anything underneath? How dare you keep my cunt exposed for others, hm?" With every seething word, I leaned in until she was pressed flat against her bed with my face inches from hers. "Answer me," I demanded, shoving my fingers deep into her sweet spot, making her whimper out a moan.

Tightening the hands and tentacles around her, I kept her squirming body pinned to the bed as I locked my hardened eyes onto her shaky ones. "Y-yours? It's my body, my pussy—ah!" Her words cut off with a sudden thrust of my fingers.

Smirking darkly, I grabbed her face with my other hand to steady her gaze on me. "No." I corrected her curtly while fingering her harshly. "You are mine. All of you belonged to me the night I claimed your lips with my own, marked that body of yours with mine, and filled your needy hole with my cum."

"I'm yours?"

Fuck me.

Releasing her face, I grabbed her hips and thrust myself fully into her after dissolving my pants away. I couldn't stop myself, not with the 'fuck me' eyes she gave me when I told her she belonged to me. My resolve melted completely with how her eyes lit up with such bliss like stars on a clear night.

"Kastoron!" She screamed with a deep moan as her body struggled to get away from me.

I probably should have been gentler, but my patience was nonexistent. "That's it, doll. Coat my cock with your cum." I chuckled against her lips before taking her bottom one between my teeth with a groan as I felt her orgasming cunt squeeze me more.

"Kas." She gasped between her ragged breaths. "Move. Please. I need to feel you more, please."

How could I deny her when her plea was saturated with sweet desperation?

Teasingly, I jerked my hips in small movements, not giving her half a stroke as I wanted to hear her beg more. "Want me to ruin this greedy little pussy of yours with my cock Stella doll? Hm? Fuck it and pump it full of my cum until you're constantly leaking it?" Angling my hips, I pressed the tip of my cock into the sweet spot deep within her, making her moan with a happy smile on her face as she gripped at the shadow bindings.

"Yes, please, yes. Do whatever you want me to, Kastoron. Just touch me, and don't leave me again, please." Her voice trailed out to a whisper as she looked at me longingly. "I missed you so much."

Fuck. She has that look in her eyes. Fuck.

Pulling out, I turn her around and force her onto her hands and knees before plunging myself back into her with a growling groan. I wasn't even out of her for a second, yet it felt like a damn eternity. "Do you remember your safe-word, doll?" As much as I wanted to use her to my pleasure, whether she wanted it or not, I didn't want to become a complete monster to her.

"God." She whimpered as her hips pressed back against me.

Reaching down, I carefully threaded my fingers into her hair and fist the back of her head and pulled—hard—until she gasped from the pain and dis-comfort of the angle I forced her to arch her back. "This is how you should always be for me, on your knees, ready to take me," I remarked with a snide chuckle before pulling my hips back and slamming into her hard and fast.

As I pounded into her with no mercy, I summoned shadow hands to slip under her. One hand went between her legs, the soft fingers playing with her engorged clit. While the other two went to her breasts to fondle her soft mounds and toy with her hard nipples. "Kastoron, fuck, too much."

"You can take it. I know you can." Debatable, considering how I practically jumped her with this. "Be my good girl and take it."

To be fair, I did intend to take it slow and easy because I wanted to savor her for one last time. Seeing her bare underneath her clothes tapped into some primal side of me, though. In hindsight, it was kind of extreme of me. There wasn't anyone else in the house besides us, and she did have every right to wear—or not wear—what she wanted. Still, the thought of someone possibly getting such easy access to her made me feel so much possessive anger that I snapped.

Stella's body tensed and trembled under me as I felt her walls choke my cock. "That's it, good girl, just ride it out." Her breaths came out in choked sobs as she fought to get away from me, only to stay rooted because of my hold on her hair and hip. "Don't fight it, Stella doll, just let your mind go mad to the pleasure."

As I continued to fuck her to my dark heart's content, I couldn't help but slowly creep closer and closer to her puckered hole with my thumb. "Any of your pathetic boy toys ever dared to take this sweet ass of yours?" I asked with a chuckle as I pressed the very tip of my thumb into her ring of muscles, making her yelp and try to buck her hips away.

"No! It's dirty!" She protested between her moans, craning her head as much as she could to look back at me pleadingly.

"No, it's a hole meant to be fucked and ruined just like your cunt. If I could fit in your mouth, then I would have ruined that by now, too." Well, I could use a spell to shrink myself, but—actually, maybe it wasn't a bad idea. The thought of making her swallow my cock whole and blowing a load into her mouth and making her swallow it was a very arousing thought. Besides, no one had to know about how low I'd go to get some head from my m—

No! Quit it!

"Kastoron, you're too big. You'll break my ass." She whimpered with a jerk of her body. "Not tonight, please, save it for next time."

Next time?

Not gonna lie; I wanted that even though I shouldn't. I shouldn't be thinking or yearning for 'next time' or the time after that and beyond.

Shaking the thoughts out of my head, I respected her wishes as I continued to move my hips at a punishing pace.

There won't be a next time. There can't be. This would be the last time I fuck and fill her.

If only that time would last longer, but my damn dick and balls had a mind of their own. I had already emptied my full load inside of her when I got enough sense in me to think about how to draw this out.

The faint echoes of our moans and groans filled the air in the room as the two of us remained connected and unmoving as we panted heavily.

"Kastoron?" Her tender voice barely broke through the haze of my orgasm.

Don't respond, don't respond, don't—

"Yes, Stella doll?"

Fuck.

Removing my hand from her hair, she let herself slump forward onto the bed with a groan before turning her head back to look at me with pleading eyes and a dopey smile. "Stay? Please? Hold me and stay?"

Fucking... Someone castrate me and tear my soul in half.

Chapter 19

Kastoron

AND MY HOPES OF escaping my destiny went down in flames and burned to ashes.

"Aesophedus, please, I am begging you." And I never beg.

I didn't think the damn communication mirror worked after all the time it spent collecting dust. Actually, I was surprised I still had it tucked away somewhere—I thought I broke it in a fit of rage. Thankfully, I hadn't and found it stashed away in my magical storage under Stella's bed.

Surely, I thought the king of shadows would take some pity on me.

Guess not.

"And my answer remains the same. No." The king's unamused voice meant he was done with me.

"What have I done to deserve this?" I asked with a frustrated groan, my fist pounding against the floorboards under the bed.

The stern glare from the king of shadows through the communication mirror was enough to send chills down my spine. "You better change your fucking tone before I send one of the others over there to set your horns straight," he said pointedly. "You should be kissing the feet of Lucifer and God for blessing you with a mate. Instead, you're over here whining to me like a little bitch because you're afraid of commitment. Fucking man up."

"She's a human! Hu-man! She has no business being a demon's mate!" I whispered loudly through gritted teeth. "This is a fucked-up joke, not some blessing from below and above."

Scoffing, Aesophedus crossed his arms and shook his head in disbelief. "So, would you rather become a mindless imp than accept your soulmate? Do you have any idea how absurd you sound right now? Do you have any idea how many would burn the world and planets to get the chance you have?"

Was I being a little ridiculous? High possibility, yes. But only because it was an absurd situation, in my opinion.

Running my hands down my frowning face, I exhaled another exasperated groan. "I can't. We can't. It just won't work out. We can't be mates. It's just too fucking cruel." I stammered out, my head hanging in defeat.

Chuckling in disbelief, Aesophedus rolled his eyes. "How do you know it won't work out? Have you tried? And no rule in the universe says you can't be mates with a human. Fiery pits of home, you could be mated to a damn hound according to the universe, so be lucky your mate is actually somewhat humanoid."

"Listen, I tried a relationship with a human already, and look where that got me." I bit out bitterly with a deep scowl.

Sighing softly, he gave me a pitiful look. "That was thousands of years ago. Times have changed and are different. Besides, that woman was not your mate back then, so things will be different with this human."

Frustration blew off with my huff. "How? She's still a human at the end of the fucking day. She might not be a witch, but she is still human and fragile." I didn't understand why no one could give me a straight answer.

"And what do we do with fragile things?" Aesophedus pressed with a hopeful quirk of his eyebrow.

"Don't touch them? Break them? I don't know." I flustered out my frustration and threw my hands up in defeat—well, more like waved because there wasn't much room under the bed.

A sigh of disappointment pulled out from Aesophedus's shaking head. "And that is why you are in the situation you are."

"I am still trapped in this damn place." I reminded the king curtly with a displeased scoff.

Rubbing his temples, he quickly snapped at me. "For a good goddamn reason. There's a reason why I constantly deny your request to free you, so maybe you should start dusting the cobwebs out of your head and use your brain for once." Great, now I felt like a petulant child.

"So basically, I'm going to remain trapped here until I fade to nothing," I grumbled with a roll of my eyes, not one bit happy about rounding back to square one.

"No... Well, yes, if you don't get your head out of your clenched ass." Aesophedus sighed with a scoff. "Listen, how do you even know things won't work? Have you ever tried? Fiery pits, have you even asked her what her thoughts are about the relationship or situation?"

Of course, he had to point out my mistakes and poke holes into everything. As if I already didn't feel idiotic and emotionally constipated enough about the whole damn thing. "Oh, yeah, just let me sit her down and cuddle her in my arms and go, 'Hey, so sorry for being a fucking ass to you, but you're my soulmate, so let's bind our souls and live happily ever after,' and blah blah blah. Like, yeah, that's going to go over well." I vented, letting my words trail out into a disgruntled grumble.

Yeah, like any normal human would take that well, especially from a demon who's been tormenting them since day one. At least attempt to torment. I had to admit—begrudgingly—Stella adapted and took my antics well. Actually, she has been the only one to do so.

Okay, so maybe the universe had something right, but I still hated it and refused it.

"I just... I don't want to damn her to a life with me." I admitted with a heavy sigh.

"Why would it be damnation to be soul-bound to you? Yeah, you're a little immature brat sometimes, but you're a good demon with a good heart underneath. You just have to pull your head out of the tar and grow up." Aesophedus said with a huff and roll of his eyes. "You need to stop letting the past affect your future."

Sighing heavily, I ran a hand through my hair and gripped my horn to pull at it. "Are you sure—"

A pointed glare was all Aesophedus needed to silence me. "I am not going to splice your soul and magically lobotomize and castrate you so that you don't have to deal with your own emotions." Scoffing, he let out a ridiculous chuckle, "And do you have any idea how much shit I would get from everyone by giving you a cop-out like that because you wanted to deny your soulmate?"

"Well, it was worth a shot..." I grumbled with a scowl. "I'll just avoid her for the next few decades then."

"Yeah, good fucking luck with that." Aesophedus laughed before cutting our connection.

Great. Just. Fucking. Great.

Laugh it up world, because you really fucked me over with this one.

A fucking human soulmate.

Fuck me.

Chapter 20

Stella

1 week later

"Kassie... Please talk to me?"
Why does it hurt so much?
God, I felt so stupid lying on the ground with half my body under my bed and talking into the emptiness. But I couldn't think of any other way to try and get through to him. Kastoron moved around the house and property freely, but he always came back under the bed at the end of the day.

"I miss you, please." This was so fucking pathetic, but I have stooped to this level.

One week, that's how long I have gone without direct contact with Kastoron ever since that second night we slept together. And I felt utterly broken. He still did things around the house, like throw small items at me, slam the doors, pound the floor, and trip me using shadow ropes, but never once had he fully manifested himself before me since that night.

I missed the damn bastard, so much so that it physically ached my heart. I don't know what it was exactly, but I felt a strange connection to Kastoron. I mean, it might have already been there since he pounced on me on my very first night here. He terrified the shit out of me, but after the initial shock, something bloomed within.

As annoying as he was, I looked forward to his antics and found comfort in them. Also, probably a little fucked up, but it also meant he paid attention to me and still thought about me enough to be around me.

Even if his antics kept up over the past week, it wasn't the same without him being present. Literally, a piece of him was missing—at least, that's what it felt like to me.

The only time I actually felt his presence was at night, but at that point, I wasn't sure if he was real or if I was dreaming. I could feel the wispy touches of his shadows, and often, the roughness of his fingers or the soft scrapping of his nails followed. Most of the time, I felt him linger around my hands, but other times, I would feel his touch wander my body—no, he hasn't tried to have sex with me while I slept. Although, not gonna lie, low key wished he would sometimes when he touched me too much and got me aroused.

It sucked to fully wake up all horny without him around to relieve me. Well, it sucked to wake up and not have him there, but it was slightly more irritating with the ache between my legs.

Disappointed at the silence I got in response, I lightly patted the floor before scooting myself back out. "I'll leave you lunch on the table again. I got a shoot to do, so don't bother me for the next few hours."

Hint hint: fucking bother me, so I know you still care!

For the most part, he didn't bother me too much when I was with a client ever since I started my home studio. I mean, he still poked his head in every now and then and messed around a bit, but nothing too major that would scare my client away. Thankfully, my client today was a close friend of mine who knew a bit about my permanent house guest. So, even if something did happen, hopefully, she wouldn't take it too hard.

Unfortunately, the session went smoothly, and I was about to lose all hope until I noticed something off with my friend. "Is something a matter?" I asked warily as I followed the direction of her gaze, which led me to the hallway.

Shaking her head, she rubbed her eyes a bit. "I... Uhh no, it's nothing. I thought I saw a shadow move, but it was probably just my eyes playing tricks on me." She dismissed me with a quick smile and a wave of her hand.

"Huh? Oh, that's probably just Kassie." I responded to her with a hopeful smile.

"Kassie? Is that what you're calling the demon who lives here?" Her eyes bugged out at me as if I had sprouted a pair of wings.

Chuckling, I reassured her with a smile and a dismissive wave of her hand. "Don't worry about Kassie, he likes to hang around—"

Bang!

"Holy shit!" My friend exclaimed to the sound of the door slamming.

"He's just throwing a fit, don't worry about it. He does it all the time. I mean, I'm surprised these doors haven't fallen off their hinges yet with how much he slams them." Okay, now I sounded like I belonged in a psych ward.

Given how my friend eyed me right now, I was prepared for her to reach for her phone and call for someone. "Do you need me to call a priest? A medium? Demonologist? I mean, you've seen those paranormal shows with me and the other girls. You know how this shit plays out."

"Gracie, it's fine. Kastoron is harmless."

Clang! Clang! Clang!

"Hey! I just got those pots!" I shouted towards the kitchen in response to the sounds of my pots and pans banging together as they fell to the floor.

Grabbing my shoulders, Gracie gave me a shake while looking at me worried. "Why are you so nonchalant about this!? You have a demon. Demon! De-mon! In your home. You should not be this fucking chill about it. Seriously, you need—ah!"

A sudden gust slammed into us, and Kastoron appeared right next to me in his shadowy humanoid form, looking as menacing as ever as he loomed over both of us. "What are you trying to say, human?" His voice was so raspy and scary that even I got chills down my spine.

Spinning around on my heel, I stick my chin up at him with a soft glare. "Kassie! Don't scare her like that. What is wrong with you? You can't just ignore me for a whole week and then pop out of nowhere being an assholey jerk to me and my friend." I probably shouldn't be squaring up to a demon, but he wouldn't harm me... Right?

"Well, I don't like your friend's tone." Kastoron bit out with a soft growl.

Placing a hand on his chest, I attempted to shove at him, but he remained grounded like a damn statue. So, I settled for feebly hitting at his chest. "Well, that's not a valid enough reason for you to get all shadowy and creepy out of nowhere." Scoffing, I rolled my eyes at him. "Go back under the bed. We'll talk later."

Growling, Kastoron's hand shot out and grabbed my neck while shadow tendrils wrapped themselves around me and Gracie. The shadows kept Gracie's protesting figure rooted while mine was pulled up close to Kastoron's-possible-glaring face. It was hard to tell his facial expression when he had it hidden behind his veil of shadows. "Need I remind you of your place with me?" He seethed inches away from my face after leaning down.

"You don't get to do jack shit with me after ghosting me for a damn week. You can't just fuck me and leave me hanging like that, you fucking asshole." My angry words came out eerily calm despite the raging storm underneath my heaving chest.

"You what?!" Gracie exclaimed, giving me a shocked look that I caught out of the corner of my eye.

Ignoring my friend, I continued to press into Kastoron, venting my pent-up emotions out on him with every word. "I don't fucking understand you. First, you terrorize me, then bully me around my own house when that plan failed, then annoy the shit out of me with your stupid antics." Inhaling sharply, I struggled against the shadow restraints because I had the urge to shove at him, slap him across the face, or both.

"Then you go and kiss me and fuck me and fuck me up." The memories of our nights together cracked at my tough shell, making my voice crack as I continued to speak. "You... You have any idea how much you hurt me? You can't just make love to me and then leave me like that." The two times we were intimate with each other came nowhere close to making love, but the unexplainable connection I felt made it feel like so.

Breathing in and out shakily, I tried to hold back my tears to no avail. "I don't know what's going on, but I just have this strong pull towards you. And what's more crazy is that I don't even want to fight it."

Sighing, Kastoron released me from my shadow restraints and pulled me into a tight hug. "Oh, Stella doll." He murmured against my temple before pressing a long kiss—I think—against it.

But then, just like that, he vanished again.

Only this time, I couldn't remain strong.

The moment his arms and body no longer supported me, I went down into a sobbing mess with only Gracie to comfort me once she was free of her restraints.

"Stella... Please tell me what I just heard isn't real? Please tell me you're not really involved with a demon like that." Gracie's worried eyes desperately searched mine for a confirmation, one she wouldn't get.

Sniffling, I quickly wiped my tears away and moved to the couch with her. "I-it just happened. We didn't plan it or anything. We just kissed one day, and then things took off. I thought things would be fine because he seemed into it, but... I don't know." Maybe I was utterly stupid and blind. "I just... God, I feel stupid."

With a pitiful smile, Gracie took my hands and rubbed them softly. "Stella, sweetie, you're not stupid. He's a demon, and he played you. Just... Let's look at priests and demonologists or whatever and get his ass booted." She suggested in a playful voice with a brightening smile, making me chuckle a little.

"Can't get rid of him, and don't know if I want to." Okay, maybe it sounded a little fucked up, and maybe a little Stockholm syndrome-ish, "Life would be a little too boring without him around. I don't think I can imagine my life without Kas in it."

Gently, she grabbed my shoulders and squeezed them. "But sweetie, you can't live a life filled with pain and heartache because your demon roommate is an asshole. I don't want you to get hurt again because of an unhealthy relationship." Gracie's deep frown was filled with worry.

With a sigh of defeat, I leaned forward and laid my head onto her shoulder. "I'll do something in a week if there's no improvement." I strained out with an aching chest. "Can we not talk about my bad relationship choices anymore?"

Sighing softly, Gracie hugged me tightly, and we remained like that for a little while until she spoke up in an awkward voice, "So, you really fucked a demon?"

Unable to help it, I let my amusement slip out in a chuckle as my face brightened up a little. "Yes, I fucked a demon... Well, more of a demon fucked me, but close enough."

Snickering, Gracie gave me a knowing look and a devious smile. "How was he?" Glancing around, she blushed and pointed between her legs, "Ya know."

Now, I couldn't help but let the heat flood my cheeks as I smiled like a goof at the memories of his demonic cock inside of me. "Huge, like," I grinned ridiculously as I did my best to measure him out with my hands for Gracie to see, "Huuuuuge. And his dick has ridges on it, and my lord do they feel amazing."

Squealing and giggling like a schoolgirl, Gracie kicked her feet and shook me excitedly. "Do you think all demon dicks are like that? Oh man, it sounds like you're living a fantasy porno!"

Rolling my eyes, I playfully smacked her arm. "I don't know how I'm not dead by demon dick, but I don't care. I mean, if all demon dicks are anything like his, then, well, I'm never going back to a flimsy human dick again." Honestly, she put out a good point. How was I not torn in half by having sex with Kastoron?

Raising an eyebrow, I tilted my head at Gracie, "Don't tell me you're going to go summon a demon just for a good lay now." That would be something I could see her doing, knowing how adventurous and crazy my friend was.

Waving her hand dismissively, she scoffed warily, "Oh please, that's too much work to be able to summon, contain, and control a demon." Well, she sounded too comfortable with that fact.

Then, she grew serious again with an unsure smile. "For your sake, I hope this Kassie demon gets his horns untwisted."

Yeah, I hope so, too.

God, please help this situation.

Chapter 21
Stella

1 week later

"Kastoron, please, I can't do this anymore."

Another painful and awful week had passed since Kastoron last held me and left me broken. I shouldn't be hung up over him, but the thought of moving on with anyone else physically pained me.

So, here I was, being a depressed lump in bed, hoping to everything holy and unholy out there to answer my prayer to send my demon back to me.

My demon. Be fucking real Stella.

Kastoron wasn't mine, but deep down, I wished he was. Crazy as it sounded, it felt like he should be mine.

I couldn't feel his presence, but I hoped he could hear me somehow. "Please, can we talk," I begged in no particular direction.

Dead silence.

I hated this silent, invisible lover shit from Kastoron. I mean, it was one thing to fuck me and act like it never happened, but to avoid me while still doing shit around the house was rude. Then, to act like he gave a damn the other day with Gracie was another knife twist to my aching heart.

The thing was, I really just wanted to talk to him about this whole matter. I had no intentions of pushing him into a relationship or anything; I really did wish only to address his response and our standing with each other. I mean, if he wanted to have some kind of friends-with-benefits situation with us, fine, whatever, just stop treating me like shit afterward. No strings attached? Kay, fine, again, quit treating me like crap after screwing me stupid.

Would it be great if somehow we had a productive and beneficial talk that resulted in us starting some kind of healthy relationship with each other? Yes, it would be very great.

But I was desperate and hooked on Kastoron, and I would take whatever I could get.

I sounded stupid, but as I said before, there was some kind of pull I had towards him—a special connection. That was the other thing I wanted to talk to him about because something about him brought a certain life to me.

"Kassie... Please..." My voice cracked as memories came flooding in along with bad feelings. "Don't hurt me like the others have. Don't be like my douchebag of an ex and fuck with my feelings like this, please."

I felt stupid for shedding some tears over this matter. "You can't just warm your way into my heart, give me mind-blowing sex and sweetness, and then just leave." Scoffing angrily, I laughed at myself a little. "If you just wanted to fuck and dump, then you should have just taken what you wanted without getting me to lower my walls for you."

I didn't do one-night stands, but at least if I knew what I got into, then I could better prepare myself for the aftermath. With how tender Kastoron was with me that night, I went into it thinking something more would come out of our relationship.

Well, jokes on me.

Talking to the air would get me nowhere. Maybe I should go to the library and look for a book on how to summon a damn demon and pull his ass out myself.

Sighing heavily, I tucked the idea away for tomorrow as I felt myself drift off from my exhaustion.

Then, just like every night, I felt his faint caress. Only this time, I fought my drowsiness enough to wake fully.

He won't escape me this time.

The moment I felt his fingers brush my palm and lace between mine, I reacted, tightening my hold on him until I had him in a vice grip.

Leaning over the edge of the bed fully, I peered down at his stunned face that looked up at me.

"What are we?"

Chapter 22

Kastoron

HOW BAD WOULD IT be if I just disappeared right now?

Besides it being cowardly, and a big hit to my pride, at least it would save me from having an awkward talk with Stella.

Okay, maybe if I really thought about it like that, it sounded stupid and pathetic of me.

Sighing heavily, I reached my other hand up to cup her sad face with an apologetic look. "I am so sorry for your tears." I never thought I'd ever say that in my life. "I am sorry for the hurt I have caused you because of my own cowardice." Slowly, I slid out from under the bed and crawled under the sheets next to her.

"Kastoron, please, just talk to me. I'm so confused and hurt, and I just want answers to what has been going on with us." The weight of her broken plea felt like an anchor dragging me down to the frozen depths of the ocean—or the fiery pools of fire of home.

Wrapping my arms around her soft body, I pulled her flush against mine. "I am so sorry for being the cause of it all. I was being a coward and was trying to run away from my problems and my feelings. I was too afraid to accept the fact that someone so precious and perfect like you is my soulmate."

I could feel her body tense in my arms as her head peeled back to look up at me with furrowed brows. "What?" Confusion and anger of some kind hardened her soft brown eyes until they made me want to pull back to avoid the lashing I sensed to be coming.

Stella's nostrils flared with her heated exhale as her eyes narrowed at me angrily. "You've been a total asshole to me because you caught feelings for me and didn't want to accept them? I'm not even going to touch on what you said about me being a soulmate. I want to discuss your issue of being as emotionally constipated as a teenage boy." Her finger jabbed at my bare chest with nearly every word until I couldn't help the deep frown from pulling at the corner of my lips.

"It would have been one thing for you to disappear completely. At least then, I wouldn't have to deal with your weird silent treatment or wonder if I did something wrong this whole time. I mean, you fuck me, screw whatever sense I have out of my system, hold me so tenderly, and care for me, then nothing, just nothing." Seething breaths heaved from her chest before more anger-filled words slipped out of her plush lips. "You throw your little fits but refuse to show yourself fully. You visit me at night but refuse to be with me fully. You touch me but refuse to let me return the affection."

The anger in her voice faded to sadness as her voice slowly cracked with each tear that streaked down her cheek. "You left me. You left me so lonely, hurt, and broken. I wanted you, needed you, but you refused to come." Her hands slapped my chest and remained there as the tips of her fingers slowly dug into my pecs.

I didn't know what else to say or do right now besides apologize profusely to her and hold her tightly. "I am so sorry." I apologized with genuine remorse.

Sitting up with my back against the bed's headboard, I pulled her into my lap until she straddled me. Unable to help it, I took a moment to take in her precious beauty under the moonlight that shone through her window.

Cupping her face, I brought her lips to mine, kissing her passionately with a shudder. My heart felt like it would explode out of my chest with how much I poured into the kiss. All the affection and desire I felt for her was dumped into this soul-shattering kiss. "Stella doll," I whispered heavily against her lips.

Leaning my forehead against hers, the two of us looked deeply into each other's eyes deeply in a peaceful and understanding silence for a moment. "I will never do that to you ever again, I swear on my damned soul. I swear, I will be the soulmate you deserve from here on out. I will never let you go. I will always be there for you, no matter what. I will not run away, never again. I will spend the rest of our lives apologizing to you for the hurt I have caused you recently." Yeah, I definitely had a lot of groveling to do, but I wasn't too worried about my methods of apology.

Stroking her cheeks with my thumbs, I appreciated her bright smile with my own grateful one as I looked at her adoringly. "I swear, I will give you all the love and affection you deserve and more, and I swear to always treat you right and do right by you." Kissing her deeply once more in hopes of swaying her, I let our lips melt together until Stella hit my chest to be let up for breath.

"So, please, will you let me? Will you please give me one more chance?"

For some reason, the thought of her rejecting me because of my stupid actions gnawed at my heart and threatened to break me completely. The thought of life without her tore at me greatly after I accepted that she was my soulmate, but this anticipation trumped it by far.

before, after the fact of her being my soulmate, already tore at me considerably, but this anticipation trumped it by far.

I guess I was somewhat fine with the distance before and removing myself because I didn't know her decision and thoughts about a relationship between us. The idea of rejection would be far worse than being cursed to this place by my ex-lover.

Her silence did nothing to my anxious nerves as I searched her eyes and face for an answer.

"Stella doll, please, answer me? I swear, we can do whatever you want, and I'll let you do whatever you want to me. Just please answer me."

Chapter 23

Stella

I SHOULD BE SLAPPING him across the face and yelling at him, not debating my options about whether or not I should entertain a relationship between us.

"What are soulmates to demons? Answer that first. Because my understanding is that soulmates are just two people destined to be together." If that was the case, was he only doing this because of some stupid destined fate?

As much as I wanted Kastoron, I wanted him to want me as well. I didn't want him to be with me because we were destined, prophesized, or some shit like that. It also made me feel icky to think of our potential relationship built on that notion.

Confused, Kastoron blinked at me mindlessly for a second before answering me, "Yes? No? I mean." Stopping, he cleared his throat and shook his head as if to clear it. "Yes, soulmates are two people destined to be together in a way, but it's much deeper and complicated than that."

Taking a deep breath, he ran a hand through his hair and looked at me with a serious face but intrigued eyes. "Soulmates are two souls determined to be together by the big guy in the sky and Lucifer himself. In a way, to you humans, it's kind of like having that one special someone out there for you. Essentially, it's the same idea, but soulmates are literally your other half."

Smiling happily, he ran his hand down the side of my hair. "Your life won't feel right or completely whole until you two end up together. Yeah, divine intervention plays into the feelings of passion and desire a little, but soulmates are also literally made for each other. Personality-wise, hobbies, dislikes, habits, and every little thing are tailored to each other to be the perfect pair."

Chuckling softly with a shake of his head, he laid his head on my shoulder and breathed me in deeply. "I felt a draw to you the moment you came in for the house tour, but I denied it and played it off as excitement after so long. I kept lying and deceiving myself because I never thought I would have a soulmate. It only really started to hit me the day I kissed you for the first time because I was annoyed."

Burying his face into my neck, he let out a deep sigh. "Granted, I was still a bastard to you after all of that because I refused to come to terms with my own emotions. As much as I hate to admit it, I was emotionally constipated, as you put it." He admitted with a sheepish chuckle.

"If you're worried that I'm only doing this now because of some string of destiny then you better burn it into nonexistence. I want to be with you because you're the first human to stand up against me and actually give me a run for my money. I am also attracted to you because of your spunk, brightness, positive outlook on life, resourcefulness, adaptability, selflessness, and just how you are an amazing person overall," he sighed heavily and hugged me tightly. "It's also why I tried to find a way to remove myself from you because you deserve so much better than a demon like me."

"Oh, Kastoron, no." How could he think that? "We all deserve some good in our lives. So, what if you're an annoying demon who's been terrorizing people for centuries on end? That doesn't mean you don't deserve someone to make you happy."

I so imagined this conversation to go in a different direction. Fortunately, it didn't because I thought he would reiterate what I said in a more elaborate way and end up going, 'Yeah, I'm with you because of destiny,' and yada yada. So, I was more than glad to hear that he truly had feelings towards me.

Also, I was fucking relieved because of this newfound hope of a relationship between us being possible. At least, it seemed like the direction we were headed based on the vibes of this conversation. "As crazy as it sounds, I can't imagine my life without your annoying ass in it. I mean, could you tone down with throwing shit at me? Maybe a little, but knowing and feeling your presence around me is comforting." Smiling with a soft giggle, I turned my head and kissed the area of his head where his horn met it. "You make me feel so safe."

"Did you just not want me as a soulmate? Or why did you try to avoid me and refuse the bond?" I was genuinely curious. He seemed enamored with me, but why try to deny things in the first place unless he didn't want me and just gave in at the end.

Kastoron's shoulders fell as he pulled back and looked at me with a sad, apologetic smile. "I was afraid of being hurt again. The last time I opened my heart to a human partner, she ended up cursing me to the land and shackled my powers. She played me, used me, and discarded me in the end." He admitted, hatred underlining his tone. "It's stupid to cling onto the past, but things just came rushing back the moment I realized my feelings for you. I know you are not her or anything close to her, but I was still afraid."

Now, it was my turn to comfort him. "Kastoron, I swear, I would never think about wronging you," I spoke with a voice filled with promise and a reassuring smile. "I mean, I might ask you to move heavy shit around the studio, fetch things for me, especially if they're in high places, but I would never abuse you."

Grabbing his horns, I yank him into a deep kiss to seal my promise to him. "I will cherish you for the rest of our lives, show you how grateful I am for you to let me in like this. I will erase all the wrongs done upon you and replace them with better memories of us. Of me." Another stroke of his horns, and I pulled him back into a searing kiss to solidify it all.

"Stella doll, what did I tell you about the horns." He strained out a growl against my lips as his hands gripped my hips.

Snickering cheekily, I smirked in response as I shivered under his darkened gaze. "I didn't think you'd get that hard."

I was barely running my fingers along the length and ridges of his horns, which I've come to adore greatly.

Rolling his eyes, Kastoron slid his hands to my ass, gripping a handful of them before landing a hard spank on each cheek, making me yelp a little. "I'm going to need to spank this lovely ass of yours sooner than later before you forget your place with me." He chuckled against my lips before giving my bottom lip a soft bite and tug.

"Oh? And what is my place with you exactly?" I asked with a curious smile as I traced his lips with the tip of my finger.

With a grunt, Kastoron sent me to my back. "Under me, with your legs spread wide, and my cock fully buried inside your needy cunt until you're overflowing with my cum." He replied with a mischievous smirk as he trapped me under him.

Stroking my cheek with the back of his finger, he looked at me with such tenderness that made a warmth wash over my body. "I am going to make love to you, mark a new beginning of our relationship with each other. Then," he paused with a dark smirk as he leaned down until he was less than an inch from my face.

His next words made me shudder and clench my aching walls in anticipation as my nipples hardened with the wave of goosebumps that erupted down my body.

"Then, I am going to fuck you like I don't love you."

Chapter 24

Kastoron

THE WAY SHE SHIVERED and squirmed under me at those simple words had me wanting to puff my chest out as her scent of arousal hit me.

Chuckling, I gripped the front of her nightgown—she really loved wearing oversized sleep shirts—and ripped it off her body without any effort. "Kastoron!" She protested with an angry pout, lashing her hand out at my arm playfully.

"Oh, hush, human." I chuckled jokingly before kissing her with a soft groan.

For the first time, I don't bind her with shadows, giving her free reign of movement. Slowly, her hands trailed up my arms to my chest, then down the rest of my body and back up again.

Surprisingly, my body was very responsive to her fiery touch. Even if she ran a little chilly to me, her delicate fingers set ablaze trails of burning desire all over my body until my uncovered cock twitched uncontrollably while leaking precum. "Kastoron, please, I need you. Now." She begged me with a breathy exhale.

The feeling of her soft hand gripping my throbbing member had me sucking in a sharp breath as I let her guide me to her wet entrance. What really did me in was the lustful look of desire that darkened her usually bright, gray-brown eyes. "Kastoron, make love to me. Make me yours." She whispered needily with a sharp, gasping moan when I thrust into her.

Our eyes never left each other as I slowly seated myself fully into her, and something about it was absolutely divine. Whatever connection we had deepened immensely, as if we were reaching into each other's and touching the other's soul. Which brought a different issue to the forefront of my mind after our high simmered down.

"Are you sure about me, Stella? About us? Soulmates or not, I still want you to have your choice." I asked her with a serious look.

Chuckling softly, she wraps her arms around my neck and pulls me into a heart-melting kiss. "That should have been something for you to ask before you shoved your cock into me, but yes, I have never been more sure of anything in my life."

Kissing her tenderly, I held her hips to help her angle them as I started to thrust in and out of her with long, slow strokes. "Fuck, I don't think I'll ever get over how tight and soft you are." I groaned into the crook of her neck before peppering the area with kisses and nips.

"Says the one with the monstrous cock." She retorted with a breathy chuckle and moan. "The ridges on your cock feel so amazing like this. I can feel each and every single one of them so clearly."

Carefully, I angled my hips to press against her sweet spot with each thrust, making Stella's face twist with pleasure as her nails raked down my back. "I won't last long if you keep hitting that spot, Kas." She whimpered with a shudder.

"Don't hold back your orgasms, Stella doll. You deserve each and every one of them." I told her with a groan before capturing parted lips in a heated kiss and shoving my tongue into her mouth. "And don't you dare hold back your lovely moans either."

Tightening my grip on her hips, I picked up the force of my thrusts, jerking her plush body with each slam until she came with a face twisted in pure bliss. Then, as much as I wanted to put her in a mating press and drill into her until she was a babbling mess. I wanted to slowly drive her mad with pleasure.

Three more powerful orgasms later, I finally come into her with a groan. Then, after a quick second to recollect myself, I smirked down at her blissful face, chuckling at how fast her expression changed to a wary one.

"What's the safe-word, Stella doll?" Just because I planned on fucking her like an unhinged beast didn't mean I would disregard her completely.

"God." She replied shakily with an excited smile.

Suddenly, shadow tendrils rose from the ground and crept off the walls, lashing at her body and wrapping themselves around her.

A quick flip, and she was pinned down to the bed on her hands and knees.

Lazily, I stroked at my aching cock as I watched a smaller shadow replica of my cock fuck her freshly filled pussy while a smaller tendril collected our mixed juices and lubed her asshole up. "Kastoron, don't you—"

She couldn't finish her sentence as she was too busy screaming from my sudden thrust into her once virgin ass. "Fucking slut." I laughed with a spank to her jiggling ass as her body trembled from her orgasm. "Coming from having your anal virginity taken, how crude."

She moaned in a daze. "So... Full... Too much..." Yet her hips bucked back at me. "So much."

Grinning madly, I gripped the globes of her ass until I was sure the imprints of my hands were branded into her flesh. "Fuck." Sucking in a sharp breath, I brought my hand down onto her ass, making it bounce as the sound of the impact echoed through the room with her moan. "Like that doll? Like being spanked like a bad little slut?"

Excitement thrummed in my ears as my vision became pinpointed onto Stella. Spank after spank, my hand came down on her reddening cheeks until I heard her sobbing through her moans. Kneading her burning cheeks, I leaned down and licked her tears away before kissing her tenderly for a moment as a reminder that I still cared.

"Think you've had enough time to adjust," I remarked with a soft chuckle before leaning back up fully on my knees.

Reaching down, I grabbed a fistful of her hair to yank her head back and used it as leverage to pull her back onto my hard length as I wasted no time pounding into her re-lentlessly. "Your ass feels amazing, so fucking hot and tight." Her cunt being stuffed with a shadow cock only made her tighter.

Groaning deeply, I slowed down my thrusts as I emptied my first load into her ass. I was far from done, though.

Honestly, I was amazed at how well she took all of it. No doubt I pressed her limits hard with this double penetration, but I didn't hear the safe-word fall from her moaning mouth. "Want to call for God yet Stella doll?" But for my sake, I had to make sure.

Stella didn't hesitate one second to reply, "No." Before another loud moan slipped from her sweet lips as her body shook from another orgasm. "I don't ever want to use his name ever again if this is how well you're going to treat me." She said with a dazed smile after craning her head more to look at me.

I grinned proudly, leaning down and kissing her deeply. "Good, because the only name that should be screamed from your mouth is mine."

A sharp gasp broke out from Stella's scrunched-up face when I thickened the shadow cock in her cunt and had it fuck her harder as I resumed fucking her ass.

"Now, scream it for all of Heaven and Hell to hear, so they know damn well who you belong to."

Chapter 25

Stella

LAST NIGHT FELT LIKE a dream come true, and I thought it was a dream until I woke up in his arms. But even then, I had to do a double take and literally pinch myself.

When he didn't disappear after I pinched myself, I smiled uncontrollably as I snuggled my sore and aching body into him with a giggle. I should probably get up and start the day, but I found it impossible to leave the comfort of Kastoron's arms.

Well, that and I was too fucking sore because, damn, Kastoron screwed the life out of me last night. Yeah, he wasn't kidding when he said he would fuck me like he didn't love me because it damn well felt like it. Hell, I'm surprised I survived the night with him.

Then, that fact brought up another train of thought.

Does he love me? Like, actually love me?

Looking up at his peaceful sleeping face, I couldn't help but trail a delicate finger down the length of his horn and face, making his face twitch and scrunch a little.

I probably shouldn't think too much about his words from last night; it was just an expression, after all, right? To fuck someone like you don't love them meant wild, crazy, mind-blowing sex.

On the other hand, we were soulmates, and he admitted that he had feelings for me. So, didn't that mean he loved me? Wasn't that how it all worked essentially? It wouldn't make any sense to me to be destined for someone and have a profoundly deep connection to them and not love them in the end.

"Good morning, Stella doll." Kastoron's gravelly voice tore me from my thoughts. "It's too early for you to make that worried thinking face. What's a matter?" He asked, looking down at me with half-opened eyes and a soft but concerned smile. "Don't tell me you've changed your mind about us." He worried with a dry chuckle.

Furiously, my head shook in response. "No, no, that's not it... I'm just thinking a bit too much, that's all. Just waking up to you like this after all the other times kind of threw me off, and it just feels kind of too good to be true, in a way. Then I just got to thinking about last night and the whole you having feelings for me and us being soulmates and whatnot."

Chuckling, Kastoron shut me up with a deep kiss. "Quit your worrying. I meant all I said last night, and I am a demon of my word." He assured me with a smile and kiss on the forehead. "How are you feeling?"

"Thoroughly fucked past six days over Sunday," I replied with a roll of my eyes while smacking him in the chest playfully. "I don't think I can walk, let alone get off the bed." I groaned playfully before burying my face into his chest.

Quizzically, I looked up at Kastoron when he started moving us off the bed. "Kas, I literally just told you I can't walk because you fucked me over with your huge dick. Why are you getting me out of bed?" Tightly, I wrapped my arms around his neck and clung to him for dear life as he stood up with me in his arms.

Slowly, he started towards the bathroom while smiling down at me. "Because I'm going to run you a bath and make you some breakfast while you relax."

"Do you even know how to cook?" I asked with a wary look, making him chuckle.

"Yes, I'm not incompetent like the lot of human males on this earth." He replied with a roll of his eyes before using some shadow hands to turn on the water and fill the tub up before settling me in. He even remembered to add in my favorite bath bombs!

Wait... I ran out of them and hadn't gotten the time to buy more yet. "Kassie, where did you get these bath bombs from?" I quickly spun around in the tub to look at his retreating body.

Stopping at the doorway, he looked back at me with a cheeky grin. "Don't worry about it." He dismissed me with a wave of his hand before disappearing completely from the room.

"Wait! Are these the ones I couldn't find three weeks ago!? Kas!"

Chapter 26

Kastoron

"QUIT ACTING SO DAMN surprised that I can cook."

"Well, can you blame me? I never see you cooking for yourself or eating anything, really. I mean, before I started leaving food for you, I wondered if you even ate, period." Stella remarked with a playful scoff and roll of her eyes.

"I usually hunt the animals around the property when you're asleep or dig into my own stash of food. Your measly portions aren't near close to filling for me, but they are a nice gesture." Giving her a fond smile, I held up another piece of bacon to her mouth the moment she finished chewing.

"No one's fed me since... Nearly forever." I appreciated her kind gesture of cooking me food when I didn't even mention anything about it.

Begrudgingly, she ate the bacon. "You're going to keep me pudgy." She muttered with a soft pout.

Sighing heavily, I reached over and grabbed her to pull her off her stool and into my lap. "You are not pudgy. You are not fat or chunky or any of those stupid terms. You are perfect just the way you are. You have the perfect amount of meat and muscles on you to make you soft and plush enough for me, and your figure is filled out perfectly. I don't give a shit what everyone else tells you, and you shouldn't either like how you advise your clients about loving their own body."

Cupping her face, I brought her full attention to me. "You are perfect, and if I hear you say anything negative about your body starting from here on out, I will start tallying it to punish you. Am I clear?"

Gulping, Stella's eyes widened a bit in wonder and fear as her head bobbed up and down quickly. "Yes, sir, understood."

"Good girl." Smiling, I leaned down and kissed her softly. "Now, finish breakfast, and we'll talk."

We still had much to discuss regarding our relationship moving forward, and we still had a lot to unload to each other about our lives. I wasn't too keen on talking about my past, but Stella questioned it earlier in the bath. I could be a jerk and dismiss her completely, but I had to be open with her if I wanted this relationship to work.

Once Stella was full, the two of us ended up on the couch with the TV on some crime documentary as background noise and as a means for Stella to relax a little before we started our serious conversation.

"Last night, the thing about the soulmates, there's quite a bit I didn't touch on that I need you to know before you absolutely commit yourself to me." I started, nervously scratching at the ridges of my horn as I ran through things in my mind.

"What? Do I have to sell my soul to you or something?" She joked with a nervous chuckle as she got comfortable in my arms.

Scratching my temple with a finger, I shrugged a bit. "Kind of? Like it's... You know what, just let me explain things from top to bottom, then if you have any questions then you can ask them, otherwise we'll be spending forever on the subject. Alright?"

Warily, she reluctantly agreed with a soft nod of her head before turning her body around to face me fully.

Quickly, I brushed over what I initially told her about soulmates last night before starting on the new information once she didn't give me a confused look. "Humans have a marriage, and soulmates have a similar thing called a soul binding ceremony, typically performed by a higher entity like Lucifer, a prince of Hell, the archangels of Heaven, or God himself. It's seldom that a pair of soulmates don't have the ceremony performed, and usually, the reason is the loss of one or the other. Either way, the ceremony is much like a marriage ceremony. Only with our vows will we literally have our souls intertwined and bound. We will become one in a spiritual sense. Until death do us part, literally. We will become each other's everything and nothing. Life will mean nothing without one or the other."

A moment of silence fell upon us as I let Stella digest the information. "So, we're like going to be really close to each other then if we go through with the ceremony?" She let out a dry chuckle to try and ease the tension from her body. "I mean, it doesn't sound too bad. Just marriage, basically, only very serious."

"Yes, marriage as it should be in its sacred sanctity." I chuckled softly as I petted her head. "But with the soul binding, we will be fully opened and exposed to each other. We'll become in tune with each other. We'll be able to feel what the other feels, hear each other's thoughts, and we can even communicate telepathically. We'll have to learn to shut each other out for some peace and privacy, and for moments we want to surprise one another, but that will be a problem later if you decide to proceed with the ceremony."

I couldn't help the happy smile from spreading on my face at the thought of us becoming one. I only hoped Stella would agree. A soul binding couldn't happen unless both parties were willing without any coercion or force. So, even if I wanted it, I couldn't drag Stella to the altar basically and force her to mingle her soul with mine, not without dire consequences that ranged from becoming a zombie of a demon or death.

"Do you want to be with me? Like, actually want me because you personally do and not because of this soulmate bond." Stella asked with a worried frown.

Grabbing her face, I kiss her deeply and passionately. "Never doubt my love for you. I have come to love you for who you are as a person, and I love how much you compliment me as a person." I spoke in a heavy voice filled with all the affection and truth I had in my body.

Stella's eyes sparkled as the corners of her lips slowly curved into an uncontrollable smile. "You love me?"

Kissing her with a soft chuckle, I held her face lovingly. "Of course. Like I said, I have liked you since you first moved in. I just didn't know how to properly get things through to you because I was an idiot. I won't throw those three dreaded words at you yet, though, until you are ready. I know how you humans like to take things slow when it comes to relationships and feelings and shit." Looking deep into her eyes with my own affectionate ones, I stroked her cheek with my thumb.

"So, you want to do the soul binding ceremony with me? I don't know why, but from how you were placing things on me saying it's my decision and all, it made it sound like you weren't really in it." Stella worried her bottom lip between her teeth as she averted her eyes from me.

Thinking back on my words, I could see how she could have mistaken it. "Oh, Stella doll, no," I assured her with an apologetic smile.

"I want to do it, the ceremony," Stella told me confidently with a determined grin that lasted a second before it turned a little unsure. "Well, maybe not like now, but like in the future, like a few months or something."

Amused, I let out a chuckle and kissed her forehead. "Whenever you want, just let me know."

Then came the moment I dreaded. Even though I was ecstatic about the fact Stella agreed to be mine and to the ceremony—in time—it wasn't enough to keep my mood up for the next part. Unfortunately, it was unavoidable.

With a sad smile, Stella reached out and stroked my face with a soft smile. "Kastoron, you don't have to talk about your past if you don't want to. We're at a good spot right now, and I don't want this moment to be ruined because of the past."

I knew better, but I was also too cowardly.

"Thank you. I promise, some other time."

Hopefully never, but that was too much to hope for.

Chapter 27
Stella

3 months later

"Kas, not that I don't appreciate the gifts, but where the fuck are you getting the money for all this shit? You better not be spending my money without me knowing, this camera is expensive."

Three months have passed since we started this relationship of ours, and every day was perfect—and every night.

It was strange to be in a relationship again after so long, and I was afraid of messing it up because of my inexperience. Thankfully, Kastoron has been more than willing and patient.

"Don't you humans like gifts? And what makes you think it's your money I'm spending?" Kastoron remarked quizzically, not bothering to move from the couch where he currently lounged on in nothing but a pair of gray sweatpants.

One of the major changes Kastoron has made thus far was his lack of clothing. Yeah, it was neat that he could fabricate his own clothes with shadows, but I wanted physical clothing on him to prevent any accidental flashings when he got too comfortable or forgot to make clothes. He wasn't too thrilled about it, but he caved pretty quickly when I mentioned being able to actually strip him and touch his body more.

"Kastoron, this is overboard in terms of gifting. I mean, some people might like this, but I'm more simple and like smaller things like a bouquet of flowers or like a cute hairpin. Hell, even a new blanket would make me more than happy." I elaborated with a long sigh as I rubbed at my temples. "And where else would you get money for this stuff? You don't have a job last I checked, so between the two of us, only I have a bank account that is useable."

I had some funds stashed away, but if Kastoron went crazy like this, then I would be close to being poor and broke.

"You do not need any more blankets, woman. You already have a whole closet stocked full of them that you don't even touch, nor do you need any more mugs for your coffee addiction." Kastoron pointed out with a playful scoff and roll of his eyes. "Seriously, you humans are worse than greed demons when it comes to hoarding sometimes, I swear."

Unable to rebut him, all I could do was cross my arms and look at him mockingly. "W-well you still haven't addressed the part about where you got your funds for this stuff." Hopefully, the change in subject won't make my wallet hurt.

Averting his eyes from me, he snapped his fingers, and a shadowy hole appeared on the ground by his feet. From the hole emerged a few large boxes filled with... Wallets?

Confused, I eyed him warily as I approached the boxes and dug through them. "Where the hell did you—holy shit, why the hell do you have a wallet from the 1800s!?" More importantly, why the fuck were there so many wallets!?

"What? You asked where I got my money from. I mean, not like these people are missing it much. Besides, they should have looked harder for their shit when it went missing if it was that important to them." He said with a nonchalant shrug of his shoulders.

"You can't just steal from people, Kastoron! That's not right." I scolded him with an angry pout before grabbing a throw pillow off the couch and hitting him with it.

"Wha—hey!" He protested, holding his arms out to block the pillow. "I'm a demon. I don't give a shit about morals and rights and wrongs. Everything is in the gray zone to me."

Continuing to whack him with the pillow, I spat my words out through the hits. "Man, I'm going to have some crabby ass guy named," I had to pause to peek at the name on the documentation again, "Richard haunting my ass because you spent the dead man's money!"

Rolling his eyes, Kastoron snatched the pillow from me and hugged me tightly with a chuckle. "You are so adorable."

He teased with a laugh. "No ghost would dare come near a home with a demon present, lest they want to be used or sent fully to the afterlife to be judged and placed where they belong."

Nuzzling his face into my neck, he tickled my sides with his clawed fingers, making me laugh away my slight anger towards him. "Silly human, worried about some stupid hauntings while I'm around... As if I could go anywhere anyways." It was hard to ignore his voice trailing out with his sad smile.

Snuggling into him, I held his hands in mine and brushed over his knuckles with my thumb. "Kas, why are you stuck here? You've mentioned being trapped here a few times, and we've always kind of danced around the subject." He didn't get explosive mad when his situation with the house was brought up, but it dampened his mood greatly.

Sighing heavily, he rested his chin on my shoulder and softly stroked his thumb along my inner thigh. "I came here to Earth long ago with Aesophedus, the king of shadows, to help capture stray ghosts and demons who cause more harm than good. Then, one day, a witch decided to summon a demon, and I answered the summoning out of curiosity."

Kastoron went silent for a moment before continuing. "The agreement was simple between Katarina and me. She asked and sacrificed things for me, and I carried out her wishes. As time passed, she became greedy and lustful for greater power and things, and she wanted more out of our relationship." Sighing heavily, he shook his head slowly. "I'm somewhat partially to blame for my situation because I engaged with her feelings when I shouldn't have... But when I realized things between us weren't healthy and tried to leave, she wouldn't let me. So, she trapped me in her home and forced me to remain bound to the property."

Scoffing under his breath mockingly, he stared up at the ceiling with an amused smile. "Damn witch got too cocky and ended up at the gallows when the townspeople caught her from what the others told me."

"Why didn't someone else help you? A demon buddy or Aesophedus himself?" It was sad to think about Kastoron being shackled here to this place all this time. I mean, how lonely must it have been for him? How did he not lose his mind?

"By the time word got to the others, Aesophedus commanded them to stand down, said this to be a punishment for me so that I could grow up." He scowled with a deep frown for a split second before softening back up. "I hated him for it, but if it weren't for his decision, then I wouldn't have met you, Stella doll."

Looking down at me with a happy smile, he studied me with adoring eyes. "It sucked, but I was also a brat who had no control over his own emotions, lashed out more often than not, and I just liked to screw around. Granted, I was the same until recently because even though I was trapped and supposed to learn a lesson, I still terrorized the human occupants over the years because of my resentment towards humans."

"I mean, you're still an emotionally constipated mess now," I remarked with a snicker, earning another tickle from him.

"But I'm getting better, for you." He grinned like a goof before kissing me tenderly. "Still hate that I'm stuck here for now, but I can try to convince Aesophedus when I talk to him next." His smile grew wide with excitement. "I can't wait to go on dates with you out in the world, take you places to eat, walk around the mall or parks, and just do whatever you want."

I couldn't help but smile lovingly at Kastoron when he told me what he wanted to do when he would finally be free. Although, speaking about him being out in public, "You can't go out looking like you do Kastoron, you're going to scare everyone away, and they're going to call a priest to exorcise your ass."

Kastoron looked at me for a second to see if I was serious or not before laughing softly with a shake of his head. "I can look however I want, baby. I only look like this because I am comfortable being in my true form around you."

Aww, how sweet.

Grinning with a giggle, I reached up to grab his face and bring him down into a kiss. "Thank you for coming back to me and giving us a chance."

Shaking his head softly, he looked at me with grateful, loving eyes. "No, it should be me thanking you for forgiving me and giving me a chance I don't deserve after hurting you like I did."

"I will always forgive you and give you more chances than you deserve because I love you, Kastoron."

Chapter 28

Kastoron

"... BECAUSE I LOVE you, Kastoron."

I never understood why three words could make or break a person until now. Hearing her melodic voice sounded like an angel beckoning someone towards the right path with those three words.

It had always been a silent, mutual understanding between us ever since the morning we had our talk about soulmates. But never once have we verbally said those words to each other. I thought it to be silly. I mean, how could three words encompass such feelings of passion, desire, adoration, and love one has for their partner?

This. This was how.

Over the years, I've seen humans say such words to each other, and I never felt anything warm upon hearing it or seeing the sight of love. Blasted heavens, I've seen and heard people say it so emptily to others without a thought behind the words. So, I never equated anything special to the phrase.

Well, guess I was proven wrong once again.

Shoving her down onto the couch, I turned her onto her back as I caged her between my arms. "Say that again," I demanded with a possessive growl that even surprised me.

Letting out a shaky breath, she smiled up at me excitedly and adoringly. "I love you, Kastoron. I love you so much." Her smile grew wider with each word until she grinned like an idiot in love.

Desperately, I devoured her lips in a needy kiss as my hand wrapped itself around her neck. "Again," I demanded with a grin.

"Kastoron, you'll hear it for the rest of our lives. No need to wear it out now." She giggled cheekily, sticking her tongue out at me.

Quickly, I captured her tongue and stole it into my mouth as I eased us into another kiss. "I will never grow tired of hearing it," I spoke between kisses before moving down her body.

Hiking her dress up, I rip her flimsy thong away and shove my face between her plush thighs after pressing her wide open for me. "Just like how I am never going to grow tired of this delicious cunt of yours." A surprising new addiction, one I didn't mind one bit.

Reaching down, she pressed a hand against the top of my head. "But Kas, I'm still so sore from last night." She whined with a cute pout.

Slithering my tongue out, I gave her glistening slit a long and hard lick that had her breath hitching with her bucking hips. "I'll lick and kiss it all better." Even if she held my head back, my tongue was more than long enough to lick every inch of her good before slipping into her throbbing pussy.

"Kastoron." Her hand was quick to slip around my horn to pull me closer with her sigh of pleasure. "Just be gentle, please." Her body relaxed into me with her plea.

Pulling my tongue out of her, I placed a quick kiss against her inner thigh with a soft smile. "I am going to show you how much I love you," I murmured against her before turning my attention back to her pussy.

The sweetest sounds of her angelic moans filled the area, along with the sounds of me feasting on her cunt as if there was no tomorrow. "K-Kastoron, I don't think I can—ah! Fuck! Can't come anymore." She whimpered while trying to push me away.

One last lick and I gave in to her plea. Leaning back onto my knees, I looked down at her pleasure-filled face with a satisfied grin. Gently, I fondled her soft breasts after I leaned down and took one in each hand. "Just one more baby. Think you can manage that for me?" I begged with a pout and big eyes.

Laughing softly, she weakly hit my shoulder and rolled her eyes. "Fine, but only if you stop making that face."

"What's wrong with my face?" I asked with an amused chuckle while taking off my pants.

Snickering, she reached up and pinched my cheek. "Don't ever try to pull a puppy dog face ever again. It's so creepy and weird." Smiling, she reached down and took hold of my thick member and rubbed it against her slit to slick me up before positioning it at her tight entrance.

Taking her hand away, I brought it up and kissed the back of it lovingly with an adoring gaze. Then, interlacing our fingers, I pinned it next to her head as I leaned down and thrust into her slowly while kissing her. Fully sheathed in her, I held the position for a moment to savor the feeling of her warmth around me and the deep feeling of being connected to her so intimately.

Shuddering, I wrapped my other arm around her along with some shadow ropes to hold our bodies pressed together as I moved my hips in slow strokes.

Moaning deeply, Stella arched her body into mine as her hands gripped mine and my horn. "Fucking... You and my horns." Somehow, at least one of her hands always ended up wrapped around the sensitive things. "Q-quit that." I shuddered with a strained groan when she started stroking my horn as if she was handling a cock.

"I need you to fill me with your cum already, Kastoron." She said breathlessly with a deep moan. "I'm so close. Come with me, please."

Between her begging, sweet moans, and her hand jerking my horn, I couldn't hold out for long, especially when her pussy tightened around me in a vice grip.

Groaning deep, I buried myself entirely in her right before I felt the familiar throb of my orgasm. "Stella, I love you so much." I kissed her breathlessly as I emptied myself out completely in her.

"Can't wait to fuck you full to where you'll get big with our child," I muttered against her lips with a smile as I rubbed her stomach with one hand. "If you want to have a little demon spawn with me, that is."

I was fine either way; as long as Stella was happy with our relationship and everything with it, then I would be, too.

Her response surprised me a little. "After we have the ceremony, then you can try to knock me up. But just so you know, you'll be in charge of diaper duty." Her happy, cheeky little smile wasn't what I had expected. I had been prepared for more reluctance or a dampened mood to talk about things. Not like I would complain about her response, though.

"Lucifer, I can't believe how stupid I was for not accepting my feelings and trying to push you away." All that time, I could have been living a better life with Stella by my side if I pulled my head out of my ass. I hated to admit it, but Aesophedus probably had a good point about keeping me trapped. Otherwise, I would have been a menace to human society.

"I swear, you will know heaven on earth by my side. By the time you come to pass, you will come crawling back to me because I am your paradise, not whatever is beyond those gaudy stupid pearly gates."

Chapter 29

Stella

3 months later

"Marry me."

"Huh?!?" Did my demonic lover really just propose during oral sex while he had me tied to an armchair?!

"Agree to marry me, and you get to come. If not, then I'll just keep edging you until you cave." He grinned evilly at me as he teasingly worked his tongue against my clit and entrance.

"Kastoron, what the fuck. You can't just bind me with my legs spread wide on an armchair and go down on me and demand an agreement to a proposal like that." I scolded him through heavy breaths as I tried to chase my orgasm by bucking my hips at him.

With a chuckle, Kastoron leaned back and brought his hand down—hard—on my throbbing pussy, making me flinch and yelp a little. "All you have to do is say yes, you'll marry me." He said nonchalantly with a soft shrug of a shoulder before spanking my pussy again with a feral grin.

"Wonder how long you can hold out if you're already so close to the edge. And fuck, you're just begging for me to use your cunt with how wet you are." To prove a point, he spanked my twitching pussy again and rubbed me slowly a few times before holding his hand up to my face. "Look at the mess you've made so far, and you haven't even orgasmed yet." His spread fingers glistened with my juices that clung and webbed to each of his fingers.

Leaning onto my thigh with his elbow, he rested his head. He lazily toyed with my swollen clit, occasionally slipping his fingers into me to keep me on the fine edge of explosive pleasure. "Or I can make you come until you really can't take it anymore. I mean, the thought of making you squirt and gush like a broken hose has its appeal. Then to shove your face into your own juices as I fuck all your holes until all you can do is beg me for more even when you've gone past your limit."

I couldn't tell if he was serious or not with the devilish look on his face, and knowing him, he would make good on one of the threats. "What happened to free will?" I snidely remark with a roll of my eyes, earning another spank from him.

"Kas! This isn't fair! I already agreed and set a date for the soul binding ceremony with you. Why does this proposal matter right now?" I already basically agreed to marry him with the ceremony, so a proposal from him seemed pointless and redundant since the ceremony was literally going to be an over-the-top wedding ceremony.

I figured six months into our relationship was enough time for us to start planning the ceremony. It had only been about two weeks since I told him I was ready to bind our souls and have the ceremony and whatnot. So far, we have a date set for six months from now, the anniversary of when we first met each other.

"Can you at least let me have a win? Besides, thought you humans placed so much importance on stupid marriage proposals where the man gets on his knees." Sighing softly, he feigned hurt, "I honestly thought you would find it sweet that I got on my knees like this for you and proposed."

"You cheeky asshole, you rip my clothes off, tie me to an armchair, and eat me out like a starved man to edge me nonstop. None of this is romantic for a proposal. And trust me, as much as I like you on your knees between me, not what people mean when they want the man to get down on a knee." I snapped back with narrowed eyes, tugging at my shadow restraints that remained secure.

Unamused, he held a hand in the air and conjured up a small black box. "Guess you probably won't want this then, huh?" Sighing with fake disappointment, he opened the box to reveal a platinum ring with a black and white diamond-encrusted band and a black heart diamond at the center. "Shame, it would have looked so lovely around your finger, and it would have popped so well against your silvery hair." He said in a playful tone as he leisurely waved the open box inches from my face.

"Oh, fuck you, Kastoron, that's not fair!" I whined with a pouty jerk of my body.

"I mean, if you want to fuck me, then all you had to do was ask." He laughed heartily before taking the ring out of the box.

"Kastoron, I swear, I will call upon the big guy in the sky if you don't put that ring on my finger right now and fuck me stupid." I groaned, throwing my head back against the back of the armchair. "Please, I promise I'll be a good, spunky wife and make sure your life is filled with excitement. Just cuff me with the damn thing and stuff my cunt with your cock and cum."

Chuckling, Kastoron reached up and gripped my face, forcing my mouth open before shoving his fingers into my mouth. "My, my, what a filthy mouth my future wife has." He remarked playfully as I sucked and licked his fingers. "I otta keep it busy." A dark grin broke out on his face as he summoned a shadow tentacle in the shape of a dick and replaced his fingers with it. "That should keep your mouth occupied while I claim your cunt and ass."

Letting out a muffled moan, I looked down at my hand as he slid the ring onto my finger with a proud and tender smile that lasted all for a second before his expression turned lustfully dark. With a jerk from the shadow bindings, my ass hung off the edge of the cushion, my holes perfectly leveled with his twitching length as he kneeled between my legs.

Just like all the other times before, he easily splits me open with his monstrosity. It didn't take long for him to send my body spiraling down a seemingly endless void of orgasms until my mind went numb to the pleasure. By the time I came back to reality, I was a dripping mess of fluids as he carried me to the bathroom to bathe me.

Once he was done bathing me, he settled me in bed on his lap to force me to eat snacks and drink water to replenish myself. Then, we cuddled in bed, waiting for sleep to fully take over. "I can't wait to be bound to you fully and officially have you as mine in every sense." He whispered lovingly and longingly against my lips with a sweet smile.

"Can't wait to be your soul-bound wife officially...? Soul wife? Soulmate wife?" Chuckling weakly, I barely managed a dismissive wave of my hand. "Whatever, you know what I'm trying to get at."

Chuckling softly, Kastoron gently kissed me before holding me tightly. "I love you, Stella doll, for now and the rest of eternity."

"That's a long time," I remarked with a forced chuckle. "I'm sure someone else will come along once I turn gray and old and die." A grim fact, but it was bound to happen with time.

"No one will ever come along because you are never going to die on me once we have the ceremony done." Kastoron's remarked with an aloof chuckle. "You and I are going to be stuck with each other for life, or until I die, which is never unless someone or something kills me, which is very hard to do." He said matter-of-factly with a cocky grin. "You'll share my life span once our souls are bound, so you are literally stuck with me for life."

Epilogue: Kastoron

6 months later

"Never thought I'd live to see the day our little brat Kas would have a ceremony." Valphan, another shadow prince, commented with a laugh and pat on my shoulder.

A sneering scoff came from another demon a little ways from me. "I'm more surprised at the fact he has a soulmate who can put up with his shit. Seriously, you remember all the pranks he'd pull when we were growing up?"

"Tezrias, you weren't any better yourself. Need I remind you of that?" A deeper voice sighed chidingly from behind me. I knew who it was, though, since only one person out of all seven of us had such a hollow voice—it was Zaesiel, Tezrias's older brother.

"You guys, give him a break. He deserves some peace and happiness in his life after being trapped in one place for so long." Amaldin's wise and charming voice calmed all of us back down to baseline.

Looking around the dilapidated church, I took in the sights of demons and angels who filled the pews, chattering amongst themselves while they waited for the ceremony to start.

I already took my spot at the altar with the rest of the shadow princes, sans one. "Where's Levianth?" I questioned, looking around for the last of us. Aesophedus was missing, but I knew he was with Stella right now to go over the ceremony with her one last time before things went down.

"Think he's with his soulmate in the bathroom while she's throwing up," Amaldin answered with an unsure scratch of his horn. "You ready for that, Kastoron? Morning sickness and all its glory?"

Sighing nervously, I shook my head. "No, but I don't think anyone ever is. I'll be there for her when she goes through it." Stella wasn't pregnant... Yet.

We both wanted to wait until after the ceremony to start trying for a child, so I had been more than cautious with using a protection spell and artifact on both of us to prevent any accidents. Also, Stella wanted to fully become solid with her studio move to the house and get her footing strong before shifting her focus onto other things besides her career and our relationship.

"You two gonna have children? Are you ready for that responsibility Kas?" Zaesiel questioned in a wary voice as he looked at me with a raised brow. "I don't mean to sound doubtful, but you've been the most immature out of all of us ever since I can remember."

I didn't blame him because I still was an immature asshole most of the time. Well, at least I knew how to reign it in now. I still pulled pranks on Stella to this day, stole and hid her shit, teased her clients sometimes, and acted more like a man-child—as she liked to call me—more often than not. But I knew my limits after all this time, and I knew when to be serious for Stella and the sake of our relationship.

"I've grown up, mostly. I wouldn't have entertained the idea of children with Stella if I wasn't remotely ready to step up." I assured the older demon with a confident smile before nervously fixing the collar of my dress shirt. "Is it getting kind of hot in here?"

Chuckling, Amaldin pats my shoulder and shakes it in an attempt to comfort me. "Breathe, everything will go off without a hitch, and you two will be bound before you even know it."

Levianth's sudden appearance cut into my tense nerves. "Sorry about that. Baby's not giving Emma an easy time with the morning sickness today." He apologized with a heavy exhale as he straightened out his suit jacket and took a spot amongst us.

"Don't apologize. It's not like either of you wanted that to happen," I said with a dismissive wave of my hand. "Just glad you could join us before—"

The heavy creaking of the church doors opening silenced the whole area and captured their attention. From it emerged Aesophedus with Stella next to him, holding his arm.

Yeah, I want to throw up.

Unfortunately, Stella probably won't let me live it down if I throw up at our ceremony. I couldn't calm my nerves down enough as my vision zoned in on her ethereal form, clad in a white wedding gown fit for the queen of heaven. She filled out the laced and gem-embroidered gown so well, and the train dragging behind her made her look like she was on a cloud.

Step by step, my heart raced like a fearful human's heart when I scared them. I was nervous and terrified beyond my own comprehension.

"Kastoron, do you accept your soulmate that Heaven and Hell have destined for you?" Aesophedus's question barely registered in my clouded mind as I was too lost in Stella.

If it weren't for the nudge from one of the other demons and Stella's giggle, I would have stood there like a complete idiot for the rest of eternity.

"Yes, I do." Fuck, I sounded so stupid with how stiff that came out. Damn nerves.

Shakily, I reached a hand out and took Stella's outstretched one and brought her before me at the altar. I wanted to tell her that she looked beyond beautifully radiant, but nothing came out of my mouth when I opened it. No matter how many times I tried, my words kept getting caught on my tongue.

"Kastoron, are you okay? You're acting like a dying fish." Stella whispered with a nervous and worried chuckle as she brushed her fingers over my knuckles.

Swallowing my nervousness, I warily nodded in response before offering her a reassuring smile. It'd be a damn miracle if I made it through this without passing out or making some fool out of myself.

I sucked in a sharp breath when I felt a sharp nudge on my back. "Kas, breathe. If you keep holding your breath like that, you're gonna turn bluer and pass out." Valphan whispered with a fleeting chuckle.

As the ceremony continued, I could not focus on Aesophedus's words because I was too starstruck by my soulmate, who stood there looking at me as if she'd won the lottery. I don't know how she remained so calm with a smiling face full of adoration and happiness. Pretty sure if someone took a picture of this moment, then I'd look like an awkward grinning duck while Stella looked like perfection and beyond.

"Kastoron...!" Aesophedus's booming voice made me snap out of my stupor.

"Y-yes, my king?" Shit, did I fuck up already? What did I do? Did I smile too much? Too awkward? Did I stare at her too much?

"Your vows? If you have any?" Aesophedus chuckled softly with an amused smirk as he gestured a hand toward Stella, who looked at me patiently.

Shit. Vows. Right.

Nervously, I gripped Stella's hands tightly as I let myself get lost in her sparking eyes to calm myself. "From the moment I heard your voice that day you toured the house, I felt myself truly come to life. Your voice woke me from a slumber I had lulled myself into after all these centuries. To say you are unlike anyone else would be an understatement because there is only one you out there in the world, the one standing before me as my soulmate. And I wouldn't want for anything else in the world than this moment and the day you accepted me into your life. I will forever be grateful for the one and only chance you are willing to give me."

Taking in a shaky breath, I forced my leaping heart back down before continuing. "I swore to you on that day, and I will swear to you now before everyone here and the high entities who are watching us at this very moment: I will spend the rest of our lives apologizing for my stupidity by spoiling you with every ounce of love and attention that you deserve and more. I will love and cherish you until the end of eternity, through sickness and in health, poor or rich, for worse and better, until death do us part. My life is yours from this day forward, and so is my heart and soul. I only ask that you grant me the blessing of having yours to cherish and protect in return."

I nearly had a heart attack when Stella's smile faltered, and tears started to stream down her face. I mean, what kind of idiot makes their soulmate cry on their ceremony day!?

But then, relief washed over me when she started giggling and laughing. "Kastoron, I still can't believe this is happening, given how we started off on the wrong foot with each other." Slipping a hand from mine, she quickly wiped away her tears before looking at me with a smile that would brighten up the darkest of days. "From the first night you scared the soul out of me, I knew you would be in my life for the long run. I just never imagined it would be forever, but I am ever so grateful that it will be. I never thought I would meet my match in the demon who terrorized me around my own home, let alone fall so deeply in love with you with each and every one of your antics."

Taking a moment, she stood there smiling at me with wonder. "I never knew love until I met you. Not only did you make me fall in love with you, but you made me find a love for myself for who I am. I love how you always look at me like I am the best thing you ever laid your eyes on like I am your whole world. I will forever be grateful for all your love and care for me and our relationship, and I cannot wait to watch us grow with time. I will always love you no matter what, and I will always be there for you through it all. Even when you get into your moods, I will always be there with open arms for you. Through thick and thin, in sickness and health, for rich or poor, for better or worse, until death do us part. I swear on my mortal life that I will be the best soulmate I possibly can. I will be your solace in the darkness, just like how you are the bed of shadows beneath me, ready to catch me."

Great, now I'm gonna cry.

I didn't want to make a fool of myself, but I couldn't hold the stray tears back. "I truly don't deserve you, but I am never going to let you go or take you for granted, ever," I whispered with a grateful smile.

A clearing throat drew my attention away from Stella to Zaesiel, who held out a set of rings to me in an open palm. Usually, this part didn't happen with a soul binding ceremony, but we made a small adjustment, which went off without a hitch.

Once we were finished adorning each other's fingers with the rings, the real important part of the event came along. "Once two souls are intertwined and bound, there is no going back. Do you two understand this?" Aesophedus looked at each of us sternly for confirmation before continuing. "Are you both here of your own free will? No coercion or blackmail from anyone?" And again, he waited for a positive answer from both of us before continuing. "Is there anyone here who objects to this? Speak now or stay forever silent."

When no one dared to object—thank all the unholy and holy figures out there—Aesophedus gestured for one of the others to give him the ceremonial dagger. "Are you absolutely sure and prepared? This is your last chance before things become permanent." The king of shadows looked at both of us one last time, waiting for our agreement before nodding at me to continue.

Reluctantly, I let go of Stella's hands to undo the buttons of my shirt so my chest was exposed. Then, with a deep breath, I nodded at Aesophedus, who pressed the tip of the dagger into the center of my chest, just right over my heart, piercing the flesh a bit. Gritting my teeth, I sucked in a sharp breath and grunted from the searing pain of having a piece of my soul ripped from my body.

To say it hurt like a bitch would be a gross understatement. If I had to relate it to anything, it would be akin to having every layer of my body skinned off one at a time while alive. But I didn't care much for the pain. It would be worth it in the end once I was bound to Stella. I only felt bad for her because there was no way she could be prepared for this.

With a piece of my blackish soul hanging outside my body in Aesophedus's grasp, I watched as he turned his attention to Stella, who gave him a nervous but determined nod. "Be brave, Stella doll." I encouraged her with a proud smile, holding her hands tightly in mine. "If I could take away the pain, then I would," I whispered.

Pacing my breathing, I watched Aesophedus carry out the same process on Stella with an aching heart. Seeing her cry out in pain when he pierced her soul with the dagger and pulled out a piece made my fingers itch to snatch the dagger away to stop it. "You are doing great, Stella doll. We are almost done." I smiled proudly at her while stroking her hands with my thumbs.

Carefully, both of us watched Aesophedus as he literally tied our souls together before urging us together with a firm hand on our backs. "You may embrace each other and your new life as bounded soulmates."

Immediately, I wrapped an arm around Stella's waist and grabbed her face with the other to bring her body right against mine before kissing her with all I had in me. Shudders racked my body as the feeling of our combined souls returned to our bodies. It felt so strange to have another person inside of me, but it felt so right at the same time.

'Holy shit, that felt weird.' I could hear Stella's voice clearly in my mind.

Chuckling, I looked deeply into her eyes as I held her face lovingly. *'How many times do I have to tell you, baby? Shit can't be holy.'* I couldn't help but smile amusingly at Stella's shocked reaction when I responded to her telepathically.

"Oh my... You're in my head...!" She gasped with a happy squeal.

Aesophedus chuckled and rubbed Stella's shoulder. "Welcome to the soul bound life. Good luck, you're gonna need it with this one."

Yeah, she was definitely going to need it. I haven't told her yet, but she really was stuck with me until death—my death, to be exact. Beings with lesser lives took on the lifeline of the demon or angel they become bonded to, so Stella would live the rest of her life with me until I died or she did—by means of murder because natural death wasn't a thing with us angels and demons.

'I love you so much.' She smiled so tenderly at me that my heart melted.

'And I will spend forever returning it tenfold. I love you, Stella. For now, and the rest of eternity.'

Epilogue: Stella

5 years later

"Mom! Bacon!"

My groan of complaint became choppy with the jerking of the bed as my three-year-old son jumped on it like a damn trampoline while demanding his breakfast. "Kassieeee." Throwing an arm over behind me, I whack a laughing Kastoron.

"Alright, bud, that's enough." The bed became still when the sounds of my son's feet hitting the mattress ceased. "What did I tell you about screaming at Mommy early in the morning?" It still surprised me how calm Kastoron always was with our son. Seriously, never once has he remotely raised his voice at our child.

Fucking best demon dad ever.

Smiling softly to myself, I turned my head to look at Kastoron who sat on the bed with Killian in his arms. "And just what's got you smiling like that so early in the morning after a long night?" Kastoron questioned with a curious chuckle.

I could feel him trying to push past the mental wall I had put up, but I held strong, earning a pout from him. "Meanie." He grumbled, sticking his tongue out at me with our son, who copied his father.

It took a while after we joined souls, but eventually, we learned to shut each other out of our minds. I couldn't even begin to tell you how many surprises were ruined within the first six months of us not knowing how to fully block each other out. Of course, I didn't mind it too much because seeing a scare from Kastoron beforehand worked wonders for me.

Giggling, I reached out and stroked his thigh after settling my hand on it. "Just thinking about us, our family, our life."

Life really couldn't be more perfect, in my opinion. I had a successful career as a photographer, running my own business and all, and Kastoron was the perfect stay-at-home dad to little Killian who was a ball of wonder in his own right.

Our child looked more human than a demon, though. Kastoron assured me it was normal, that Killian's demon form wouldn't start to kick in until his teen years. Apparently, it was typical for half-demon children to look more like the other parent to blend in with their society and live within it easily—it made perfect sense to me. If Killian had been a full demon, he would look like a demon.

Even though he looked more human right now, some of Kastoron's features could still be seen through Killian, especially his catty eyes, which always meant trouble. Unfortunately, my looks were all Killian got from me; his personality was nearly all Kastoron's—very unfortunate for me. The house never knew a moment of boredom with those two. I don't think I've had much peace to myself since I gave birth to Kastoron's personal trickster assistant. The two of them practically pranked me nearly every minute of every day.

I didn't mind it, of course. It was refreshing and lovely to watch Kastoron with Killian. Damn demon was so nervous about fucking up his own child that he became such a helicopter parent until I gave him a swift kick in the ass. I mean, I understood his worries—hell, I was worried about being a bad mother myself. But still, that didn't give him a right to be so uptight and overly cautious with our child to where he wasn't enjoying life.

"Thank you for gifting me all of it and allowing me to be a part of it." Kastoron leaned down and kissed my forehead, smiling at me adoringly.

"Thank you for coming back to me. None of this would have happened if you hadn't." I threw back at him with a grateful smile.

"No. Thank you for giving me a chance I definitely didn't deserve." He argued with a playful grin and chuckle.

Shaking my head, I decided to let him win this time because I was too exhausted to get into this with him this morning. "I'll make breakfast in a bit. I just need a few more seconds." I mumbled, burying my face into my pillow.

A big, warm hand rubbed my bare back. "No, rest, you need it. I got it handled like always, so don't worry." A soft kiss fell on my temple before I felt the bed shift and the sounds of footsteps exiting the room scratched at my eardrums.

Yeah, after a long day at a wedding shoot and coming home to Kastoron fucking me into the next lifetime, I definitely deserved some extra Z's this morning. Kastoron was more than competent enough to keep himself and our child safe and occupied.

Unfortunately, the small nap turned into full-on sleep because it was nearly dinner time when I woke up to Kastoron shaking me. "Holy shit, why did you let me sleep so long?" I probably needed it, but I didn't like sleeping a potentially productive day away like that. I could have been editing pictures or booking new clients!

Chuckling amusingly, he shook his head at me, "Again, shit can't be holy."

Sighing softly, he sat down on the edge of the bed and pulled me into his lap. "Stella doll, I tried earlier with lunch, but you weren't budging one bit. I nearly called the doctor, but you were still breathing, and your mind was still present from what I sensed. One day of rest isn't going to kill you, darling." He still seemed too worried for my liking.

Placing my hand comfortingly on his face, I smiled at him reassuringly. "Hey, you're right. A day's rest won't kill me, especially with all the projects I've been working overtime on." Yeah, I bit off more than I could chew—sue me. "I don't need to get the wedding photos back for a few more days anyway. So, let's plan a family outing?"

Yes, Kastoron was no longer chained to the property. Actually, turns out he was free when he pulled on his big demon pants and manned up. Aesophedus may or may not have intentionally 'forgotten' to mention it to Kastoron—whoops.

"Kas?" I looked at him questionably when he remained quiet and stared off in thought. It only worried me more when I couldn't get into his head. "Is something—"

"When was the last time you bled?" The serious question and tone came out of nowhere as Kastoron intensely searched my face for an answer.

It took me a second to figure out what he meant after my shock died down. "If you're referring to my menstrual cycle or a period as it's more commonly known, then it was..." Last month?

Right...?

... Fucking shit...

No, stop it, stop freaking yourself out. You had a period last month.

"Last month towards the end," I replied with a scoff of disbelief as I mentally scolded myself for giving myself a scare.

"What was the date?" Kastoron pressed as he stroked my hair.

Scrunching my face, I looked at him warily. "I don't know, around March 23rd." That sounded about right? Yet, why did I have this sinking feeling in my stomach?

"Doll, it's May, nearly June." He deadpanned, making the feeling turn into full-blown nausea.

Denial was quick to set in as my anxiety rose to an all-time high. There was nothing wrong with having another child, but Kastoron and I have never had a talk about expanding the family yet. The two of us were more than content with Killian and where we were in life right now as a whole.

Did he even want another child?

In my shock, I accidentally dropped the mental block between us.

'Honey, why would you even worry about that? Any child we create is a miracle and a blessing who I will forever cherish and love just as I do you. Unplanned or not, I will love them all the same.' Kastoron smiled reassuringly as he held my face. "If you are pregnant, I'll just start expanding the house sooner than later." Pinching my cheek softly, he boops my nose, "But don't worry about that for now until we get a confirmation from the doctor, alright?"

Humming softly, I nodded in response before giving him a quick kiss. "Will you still love me after I get fat again?" It was a slight worry that dangled in the back of my mind still. I might love my body, but sometimes, I found it hard during moments when things swung low. Especially after having a child, my body wasn't how it used to be.

I was curvier, with more thighs and rolls around my stomach to where I had a permanent little muffin top pouch going on. Kastoron always insisted that he loved all of me because this body was the one to nurture our child and bring him into this world. He also loved how softer and fuller I was for him to snuggle and love.

Deviously, he smirked at me and threw me onto the bed, caging me between his body. "Do we need another photoshoot?" He asked with a wickedly playful grin as he trailed a finger down my body.

"Killian is busy with Valphan's kid for the next few hours. I can easily grab the camera and summon some shadows to play with you while I get the perfect shots." He whispered hotly in my ear before nipping it and raising some shadow tendrils to sway in the air teasingly.

Gulping, I turn my gaze from him to hide my excitement. Too bad he wasn't gonna let me off the hook that easily. "Hm? Well? Don't you think we need another well-shot picture of my cock splitting your tight cunt open? I so loved how detailed your puffy lips wrapped around my length. Then, that perfect shot of your orgasming face," groaning with a satisfied growl, he grinned at me, "Fucking perfection."

"S-shut up and grab my camera."

"Atta girl, there's my good little slut coming out to play."

Afterword

THANK YOU SO MUCH for reading my very first novella! Please leave a rating if you enjoyed it and go check out my other books to support me!

I hope you guys stay tuned for the next novella in this little standalone series with the Umbra Demons as I have a lot planned and in store for more couples! Next up will be the story about Amaldin and his soulmate Gracie, who never thought she'd end up in the closet with a sexy shadow prince from hell.

Also, follow me on my social media for the latest updates and sneak peeks!

tiktok.com/@rose.chase.author

instagram.com/rose.chase.author/

facebook.com/rose.chase.author

amazon.com/author/rose.chase

About the Author

ROSE CHASE, A DEDICATED nurse and loving mother to two boys, discovered her passion for storytelling in middle school on online forums and Wattpad. Despite her busy life, she delves into the captivating realm of contemporary romance, with a particular fascination for dark romance and morally gray characters. Through her skillful storytelling, Rose navigates the intricate dance between love, desire, and the shadows of human nature. When not saving lives or caring for her family, she immerses herself in the world of fiction, inviting readers to explore the depths of love and passion while confronting the complexities of the human heart.